FOREVER WINGMAN

By

Thomas Willard

Approximately 34,000 words.

Copyright ©, Thomas Edward Willard, 2023.
All rights reserved.

Table of Contents

Introduction 1

Chapter 1 – Cutting the Gordian Knot 9

The Conundrum – Wednesday, 6 February 1952 9

All Wound Up 19

Forever WIngman 29

Three-Way Blessing 44

Seduction 66

Chapter 2 – Family Wingmen 92

A Dad's Intuition 92

Gainfully Employed 95

Dance Code 102

Road to Riches 115

Chapter 3 — 15th Year Reunion of the 55th Fighter Group: Day One 129

First Dance 129

Con Job 134

Chapter 4 - 15th Year Reunion: Day Two: Mid-Morning.......... 141

Pre-Flight Inspection.. 141

Airshow... 149

No Worries... 154

Chapter 5 — 15th Year Reunion: Day Two: Early Afternoon ... 157

The Chase.. 157

The Talk.. 159

Chapter 6 — 15th Year Reunion: Day Two: Late Afternoon..... 175

Landing 175

Wet Welcome and A Little Horse Trading 179

No More Hiding.. 184

Chapter 7 — 15th Year Reunion: Day Two Evening: It's About

Time 188

The Hermit's Announcements 188

You Taught Him the Code? 190

Thomas Willard © 2023

Thomas Willard © 2023

INTRODUCTION

Philosophers and poets have been trying to answer the question, "What is Love?" for millennia.

According to psychologists, love is a set of emotions and behaviors characterized by intimacy, passion, and commitment. It involves caring, closeness, protectiveness, attraction, affection, and trust.

They note that love can vary in intensity and change over time and that it is associated with a range of positive emotions, including happiness, excitement, life satisfaction, and euphoria. But it can also result in negative emotions such as jealousy and stress.

Thomas Willard © 2023

Some say love is one of the greatest human emotions. Yet, despite being one of the most studied behaviors, it may still be the least understood. For example, researchers debate whether love is a biological or cultural phenomenon, though the most recent research indicates that love is likely influenced by both biology and culture. And although biology may be an important aspect, the way we express and experience love is influenced by our conceptions of love.

Psychologists have identified several distinct types of love, including Friendship, which involves liking someone and sharing a degree of intimacy; Infatuation, often taking place early in a relationship and involving intense feelings of attraction without a sense of commitment, but which may later deepen into a more lasting love; Passionate love, marked by intense feelings of longing and attraction, and often involving an idealization of the other person and a need to maintain constant physical closeness; Compassionate/ companionate love, marked by trust, affection, intimacy, and commitment; and Unrequited love, when one person loves another who does not return those same feelings.

The question of whether love is biological or cultural is still being debated. Some psychologists suggest that love is a basic human emotion, like happiness or anger, while some sociologists believe it is a cultural phenomenon that arises partly due to social pressures and expectations.

Recent research, though, has found that romantic love exists in all cultures, which suggests that love has a strong biological component: it is part of human nature to seek out and find love. However, cultural norms can significantly affect how individuals think about, experience, and display romantic love.

Psychologist and biologist Enrique Burunat, the author of "Love is not an Emotion," published in 2016, thought love was not an emotion but a physiological drive, and wrote, "Love is a physiological motivation such as hunger, thirst, sleep, and sex drive."

Conversely, the American Psychological Association defines it as a "complex emotion." Still others distinguish between primary and secondary emotions and put love in the latter category, asserting that it derives from a complex mix of primary emotions.

According to psychologist Kristina Hallett, research has defined two major types of interpersonal love: passionate love, what we think of as romantic love, involving attraction and sexual desire; and attachment, also known as compassionate love, which can be between caregivers and children, long-term romantic partners, and other deeply bonded relationships.

She wrote, "We can certainly love people in a multitude of ways and often do. When we think about the different Greek words for love, it's possible to see how these connect to the greater categories of passionate and compassionate love."

The ancient Greeks used at least eight words to capture the various kinds of love.

The first of these, Eros, or passionate love, is all about romance, passion, and attraction. It describes the intoxicating and thrilling emotions that the first stages of a relationship can induce. The ancient Greeks considered Eros to be dangerous and frightening, though, as it involves a "loss of control" through the primal impulse to procreate.

The second type of love, Pragma, or enduring love, is sometimes translated as "practical love," referencing the kind of love grounded in duty, commitment, and practicality. While this might apply well to the type of love that blossoms in an arranged marriage, this is also the type of love seen in long-standing relationships and partnerships – like with an old couple that has been together for decades. Pragma requires a commitment to each other and might be thought of as a conscious choice or perhaps as the type of love that takes years to develop through bonding and shared experiences. Marriage therapist Jason Whiting notes, "The brain's response to a cherished long-term partner looks like contentment, caring, and nurturing." Hallett adds that Eros can develop into Pragma, and in fact, many romantic relationships involve both.

The third type of love, Ludus, or playful love, is flirtatious and fun, without the strings that come with Eros or Pragma. It can be seen in the initial stages of a relationship, when two people are flirting, courting, and crushing on each other. It often involves laughing, teasing, and feeling giddy around a person. It is very childlike in that way, though it can certainly evolve into something more serious.

The fourth type of love is Agape, or universal love. It is a selfless, compassionate love for strangers, nature, or God, also known as universal loving-kindness. It is the kind of love you feel for all living things without question that you extend knowingly without expectations for anything in return. It is a very pure and conscious love, where a person is willing to do anything for another, including sacrificing themselves. Agape is the love that allows heroic people to sacrifice themselves for friends in combat, but even for strangers they have never met.

Thomas Willard © 2023

The fifth type of love is Philautia, or self-love. This love is about self-love and self-compassion and is important for our confidence and self-esteem. More love of self equals more love to offer, with the Greeks saying you cannot pour from an empty cup.

The sixth type of love is Storge, or familial love. This love is shared between family members and sometimes close family friends and friends from childhood. Storge is compassionate, protective, and deeply rooted in memory.

The seventh type of love is Mania, or obsessive love. This is a toxic type of love where there is usually an imbalance of affection, causing one person to become overly attached.

The final, eighth type of love is Philia, or deep, long-lasting friendship. It is platonic, but you can still feel very close to those you have Philia toward and can confide in them, trust them, and respect them on a very personal level. According to Hallett, these friendships can be just as impactful as romantic relationships.

Plato thought that physical attraction was not a necessary part of love; hence the use of the word platonic, meaning "without physical attraction." But he also thought Philia was a greater love than Eros and that the strongest loving relationships were ones where Philia led to Eros: a "friends-become-lovers" situation.

CHAPTER 1 – CUTTING THE GORDIAN KNOT

THE CONUNDRUM – WEDNESDAY, 6 FEBRUARY 1952

Matt awoke early and, lying next to a sleeping Jeff, staring at the peaceful, beautiful face of the person he loved the most in the world, was deep in thought.

He felt enormous relief and was thankful that his prayers had been answered. But he now faced an overwhelming moral dilemma and wasn't sure he was up to it.

He knew Jeff was going to be all right physically, and all his other problems had been resolved. There was only one issue remaining, but it was a doozy: what was the relationship between Jeff, Linda, and him going to be like going forward?

Matt loved Jeff and had bonded with him even more over the Korean rescue mission and Jeff's medical crisis. What if Jeff felt the same way about him; that could only put more strain on Jeff's marriage.

The last thing Matt wanted was to be the cause of Jeff and Linda's breakup, a home wrecker. He loved both of them so much that he could never let that happen. But he thought Jeff might not be able to give him up now, the same worry Matt had that he could not give Jeff up, not after what they'd recently been through together.

Until the night before, Matt hadn't been intimate with Jeff since he'd become engaged – except for that one time, just after they'd been recalled, at Langley AFB, Hampton, VA, when they'd unexpectedly found themselves alone in the barracks' showers and Matt, overcome by the sight of a naked, soaped-up Jeff, had lost control of himself.

Thomas Willard © 2023

Matt had broken his "no sex with a married man" rule again last night to prove to Jeff that he wasn't impotent and to restore his confidence enough to try to make love to Linda again. He rationalized then they wouldn't be cheating on Linda; it was almost a medical intervention. But afterward, when his lust-laced need had been satisfied, and Matt was honest with himself, he realized he'd partly used the intervention as an excuse to be intimate with Jeff.

Suspecting his motives and knowing he'd soon succumb to temptation again – he was already perving on Jeff as he slept - Matt desperately tried to think of a plan to withdraw from Jeff's life without Jeff suspecting what he was up to and leave Jeff all to Linda.

But before he burned his bridges, he wanted to be sure that Jeff was going to stay with Linda, that he was over his impotence issue and could handle being sterile. If he were, Matt would find an excuse to leave while he still had an ounce of self-control left.

Thomas Willard © 2023

So, Matt devised a plan. First, he'd call Linda and ask her to return to Concord that evening. Matt would spend the day groping Jeff – at home and in the YMCA's pool – and get him all worked up. Then, just before Linda arrived, Matt would fake making out with Jeff, opening his clothes, kissing him on the neck, and rubbing his bare skin, front and back, under his shirt.

When he spoke to Linda later that morning, he'd let her know about his plan and warn her not to give Jeff any time to think but to pounce on him as soon as Matt left with Mikey.

If the plan worked and Jeff was able to make love to Linda, then Matt would find a reason to leave Massachusetts. One option was to rejoin the active service and volunteer for another tour in Korea. That way, he'd be gone for at least a year to give Jeff a chance to get over him, though Matt knew he'd never get over Jeff.

There were only two problems with his plan. The first was he loved Jeff so much he wasn't sure he was strong enough to last a day, let alone a year, being separated from him; where was he going to get the strength? And the second was he didn't want to leave his dad alone ever again.

So, Matt decided his plan needed a little more work and got up to take a shower: he often had his best ideas in the shower. Then he remembered a pledge he'd made to himself and needed to go to the store and buy a copy of the regional newspaper, The Globe, and search its want ads.

Soon after Matt got up, Jeff awoke. He could hear Matt in the shower softly singing, so he knew he was safe: that was now Jeff's constant concern.

Jeff had slept the best he had in years the night before lying next to Matt, which got him thinking: what was he going to do now? He loved Linda and Matt so much. How was he going to manage the two relationships?

His feelings for Matt were stronger than ever since all the Korean drama. He loved Linda and Mikey so much and was filled with regret for all the pain he'd just put them through. He was also ashamed of his failed attempts with Linda and wasn't sure he'd

Thomas Willard © 2023

ever be able to make love to her again. Adding to his feelings of inadequacy, despite Matt's confidence otherwise, he was certain he was sterile and wouldn't be able to father another child with Linda.

Matt had proved the night before that Jeff wasn't impotent. So why wasn't he able to perform with Linda? He still found her beautiful and desirable. And he loved her personality and admired her character; she and Matt were the finest people he knew. Then he realized he might be subconsciously blaming her for his not being with Matt.

Jeff loved Matt and knew he had an irrepressible need to be with him physically, but Matt wouldn't be intimate with him anymore: Matt thought that Jeff belonged to Linda, and, except for last night - and that one time at Langley when a temporarily sex-crazed Matt had jumped his bones in the barracks' showers - Matt hadn't had sex with Jeff since he'd become engaged.

Matt's unstated rule - meaning they never got to discuss it, and Jeff was left to infer it - was they could be as affectionate as humanly possible, but they could never have sex: Jeff's sex belonged to Linda.

Jeff's big mistake was in not immediately enlisting Frank's help in overriding this rule, enforced with the threat of a spanking, if necessary, though Matt had told him Frank had never spanked him, so it would be a little awkward to start then, when Matt was twenty-four-years-old. He thought Frank would have done it, though.

But now, since Korea and the past few days, Jeff's need to be with Matt was overpowering. Jeff could only think of two solutions: Matt would have to relent and resume having sex with him and more, or he'd have to leave Linda. Jeff's body and subconscious were conspiring against him and would only allow him to either have sex with both Linda and Matt, or just Matt. There was a major problem, though. Matt was not going to get on board with either option.

Suddenly tired again, Jeff thought he'd take a nap to think things over and pulled the covers over his head: his best ideas often

Thomas Willard © 2023

came to him while sleeping. But before dosing off, he remembered a lifelong commitment vow he'd tried but failed to make to Matt before their graduation and his marriage to Linda. He resolved to try again and not take no for an answer.

Frank had barely slept a wink all night. He'd tossed and turned trying to work out a solution to what now seemed an intractable problem – Matt, Jeff, and Linda's relationship - and had gone to work exhausted.

Frank thought he understood their situation: Matt wanted Jeff and Linda to be happy together, and that would mean to Matt he'd have to leave Jeff; Jeff wanted Linda and Matt to be happy, but if Matt left Jeff, they'd both be heartbroken; and if Jeff tried to leave Linda, Matt wouldn't accept it, leaving all three miserable.

Frank knew Linda loved Matt nearly as much as she loved Jeff, that Jeff had made her aware early on about his close relationship with Matt, and that she seemed to accept it. In fact, Frank thought she more than accepted their closeness; she encouraged it and had always joined Frank in smiling whenever they'd caught Matt and Jeff showing signs of affection towards each other.

Frank's only progress in solving the dilemma was remembering Spiegel's advice when dealing with a three-way relationship: all three people needed to be open and honest with each other, and they needed to ignore societal norms and invent their own rules.

The problem was, as far as Frank knew, none of the three were discussing the situation or offering any solutions. He knew they all had the same goal, though: to make the other two happy.

He had faith that Linda and Jeff would eventually discuss the problem together. But he knew Matt was a hopeless case when it came to dealing with personal issues like this or discussing his feelings openly. Maybe Jeff could get him to talk to him, but he thought all Linda would get out of Matt was a sunburn from the radiation coming from his blushing face.

Thomas Willard © 2023

Mentally exhausted, Frank returned to a problem he thought was much easier to solve, designing the J79 engine, a 14,000 pounds-force thrust replacement for the J47 turbojet.

When Linda got a call from Matt around noon asking her to come back home that evening at 5:00 pm sharp, she suspected Matt was up to something.

First, Matt had never called her at her parent's home before; and second, it sounded like he was covering the phone with his hands so Jeff couldn't hear him.

After Matt asked her permission to take Mikey home with him to Swampscott for the night and then warned her that Jeff was feeling frisky and that she should pounce on him, not give him any time to think about things, she guessed that Matt was arranging some kind of sex ambush for Jeff. Though always crazy, Matt and Jeff's schemes often worked, at least on each other, so she agreed.

As soon as she'd hung up, she started thinking about their tangled relationship yet again. She'd been thinking about little else since getting the call from Jeff saying he'd gone to the hospital with Matt and that everything was all right now.

She was devising a scheme of her own but hadn't worked out all the details. She only knew that it would be cruel to separate Matt and Jeff ever again and vowed to come up with a plan that would keep all of her family – now including Matt, Frank, and hopefully an addition – together forever. The key would be for them all to be morally flexible and embrace their set of extraordinary challenges. She'd need time alone with Jeff to plant the seed and with Frank to get his permission before the three of them could meet to conspire and come up with a plan to get past Matt's defenses.

#

ALL WOUND UP

Matt teased Jeff all day, especially at the pool. He started again in the kitchen after they'd returned from the Y. While preparing dinner, he unbuckled Jeff's belt, unbuttoned his shirt and pants,

Thomas Willard © 2023

then rubbed his back under his shirt while managing to stay out of reach so Jeff couldn't undress him.

When Linda and Mikey arrived at 5:00 pm, they both embraced Matt and a half-naked Jeff together. Matt told Jeff he and Mikey were leaving to visit Frank while still molesting Jeff's back under his shirt, with Jeff standing on one leg, holding and kissing Linda. Then, Matt reached in between Jeff and Linda and surreptitiously unzipped Jeff's pants, groped his groin over his underwear to check that Jeff was good to go, said they'd be back early in the morning, and then goodbye as he led a waving Mikey out the kitchen door.

Once in the car, Matt let Mikey know they were going to visit Grampy Yetman for the night but that they needed to make a stop along the way in Peabody first to pick up a surprise he had for Grampy, without mentioning he had the same surprise for Mikey.

When they pulled into the driveway in Swampscott, Frank, who'd just finished shoveling the snow from the sidewalk, was there to greet them.

Thomas Willard © 2023

Matt knew Frank loved Mikey but hadn't had a chance to see him for almost two years. Bringing Mikey to visit was part of Matt's overall plan to liven Frank's life up. But when Mikey climbed out of the passenger-side front seat to hug Frank, he was quickly followed by two Labrador Retriever male puppies – one blond and the other chocolate - which launched the second part of his plan.

A very exuberant Mikey, with the puppies jumping all over him, said, "Grampy, we got two! One for me, and one for you. Which one do you want?"

Frank, smiling, looking at Matt, and shaking his head, accepted he was now the proud owner of a new dog and said, "You pick. Whichever one you choose can come to visit his brother anytime."

Matt's other scheme had also gone to plan. Moments after Matt and Mikey had left for Swampscott - before the car was even out of the driveway - Jeff and Linda, still partially dressed, made love on the kitchen table.

Thomas Willard © 2023

After a moment to recover, they moved to the bedroom and finished undressing each other before climbing into bed and getting under the covers. They caressed each other to let their bodies get re-acquainted, then Jeff followed his usual practice of napping for 20 minutes.

When he awoke still aroused, he started to make love to Linda a second time, but as soon as he began, his body failed him again.

Linda, now keenly aware this would likely happen again, immediately began reassuring Jeff.

"Jeff, it's all right. No worries, OK?

"You're not impotent; you're still the same man I married. It's just that your body is upset about something, and I think I know what it is.

"You have a physical need to be with Matt. Your body has given you five years to come up with a plan to make it happen and is done waiting. You need to figure this problem out now, or you won't be able to perform again with anyone else."

Thomas Willard © 2023

Jeff, unable to look at Linda, said, "Yes, I think you're right. But Matt won't let me be intimate with him anymore. He thinks my sex belongs to you. I don't know what to do."

Linda, relieved that Jeff had opened the door to discussing the problem, tenderly said,

"I have an idea that I think will solve all of our problems. It may shock you, though."

Jeff, beginning to tear up, at a loss over what to do, said, "If you think you have a way to fix this problem, I won't be shocked; I'll be amazed and grateful."

So, Linda began to describe the outlines of her plan. The first, most important step was that Jeff needed to find a way to permanently prevent Matt's backsliding by entering into some kind of mutual lifelong commitment with him.

Jeff said, "I'd guessed Matt would behave like this, so I had a plan in the works before we got married, but my timing was bad, and it fell through. I promise I'll try to implement the plan again the next time I get Matt alone."

Thomas Willard © 2023

Then Linda dropped a bombshell.

"I think we need to be in a three-way relationship with Matt.

"I love you, and Matt loves you, so you'd be the center of attention."

Stunned but with a big smile on his face, Jeff asked,

"Are you serious? That would make me the happiest person in the world!" not realizing he'd already started to become fully erect.

Linda, also smiling, having noticed Jeff's arousal, said,

"Yes, I'm serious. I don't want any barriers between the three of us. I want you two free to show your affection and to be intimate with each other around me.

"But there's something else. I got a glimpse of the hidden, fearless Matt that you know like no one else. I understand why you love him, and I've got a crush on him now, too. And I'm curious about his body.

"I know he's not into women, but I still want him to be comfortable being naked around me. We'd have plenty to talk about, comparing notes about you while you're napping after sex.

"But I have another reason for wanting the three of us to share a bed.

"I don't care about it, but I think you're still feeling bad about being sterile.

"What if we ask Matt to be a sperm donor? I think you'd like Matt to have a chance to be a father, and it would give Frank a chance to be a granddad.

"If it's a boy, we will name him Francis Mathew, and if it's a girl, Kathryn Rose, after yours and Matt's moms."

Flabbergasted, Jeff could only hug Linda with all his might. But then reality set in, and he said, "Matt will never go along with the program. He's too honorable for his own good."

Linda, knowing Matt, agreed but said they wouldn't ask Matt. They'd run the idea past Frank, and if he gave his

Thomas Willard © 2023

permission, they'd use whatever devious methods necessary to get Matt to go along.

Jeff said, "Yes. With Matt, the less he knows, the better, at least until you get his clothes off."

As they were discussing the plan, Jeff noticed he was fully aroused and had begun leaking. Linda felt the wetness and said, "I think your body likes the plan," and started nuzzling Jeff's neck. Then they made love twice more before falling asleep for the night, with Jeff holding Linda from behind.

Around 7:30 am the next morning, Matt and Mikey arrived back in Concord.

Mikey, all enthused, was showing Jeff and Linda his new puppy, the blond-colored one he'd chosen – but really the one that had chosen Mikey, with the chocolate-colored one choosing Frank.

Matt, in uniform, was reporting that morning to Colonel Rylance at Hanscom Air Force Base in Bedford, MA, the next town over, just a few miles away.

Thomas Willard © 2023

Jeff, distracted for a moment and nearly as excited by the new puppy as Mikey, asked Matt if he'd come back after he finished reporting to spend the day with him and to stay the night: Linda was working the 4:00 pm to 11:30 pm shift, and Matt could help keep him company.

When Matt reported to Colonel Rylance at 9:00 am that Thursday, he thanked him for Jeff's recommendation to Raytheon and said he was available anytime to do anything the Colonel wanted.

The Colonel, having been brought completely up to speed by a follow-up call from Colonel Harding at Nellis AFB soon after Matt had left to catch the shuttle flight from Nellis AFB to Hanscom AFB, said he was aware of and wanted to support Matt's efforts to help Jeff any way that he could.

The only duty he wanted from Matt, and only if he had time to do it without interfering with helping Jeff, was for Matt to give an informal presentation to Hanscom's Reserves unit Sabre pilots about his experience in Korea. Anytime would be fine, but a Friday afternoon would work best.

Matt said he was sure he could pull a presentation together quickly, by the next day or the following Friday, whichever he preferred.

The Colonel thought the following Friday afternoon, from 1:00 pm until 3:00 pm, would be good; it would give him a chance to notify the members of the unit.

Then Matt, wanting to give the Colonel the best presentation he could but not sure if he'd be able to discuss the details of the rescue mission honestly, asked if he could invite Jeff to give part of the presentation.

The Colonel, aware of how modest Matt was – word had leaked out in England that he'd refused the Congressional Medal of Honor – said that was a great idea and was looking forward to meeting Jeff. Then the Colonel dismissed Matt, saying he didn't need to report for duty again until just before the presentation - Matt had more important work to do, helping Jeff recover.

Thomas Willard © 2023

FOREVER WINGMAN

When Matt returned to Concord around noon, he was warmly greeted with hugs from Linda, Jeff, and Mikey. Matt chalked all the affection up to everyone being happy about the new puppy.

They had a great lunch together, then spent a lazy afternoon trying to pick a name for the dog.

Matt noticed a closeness and tenderness between Linda and Jeff that wasn't there the day before and assumed Jeff was back to his old self. But then he noticed Linda was being affectionate with him too and thought maybe she was just grateful to him for giving Jeff a helping hand yesterday.

At about 3:30 pm, Linda started getting ready for work and, after putting her coat on, gave everyone, including Matt, a kiss goodbye.

With the report on the local news of a moose being seen in the area, it was decided by Mikey, with a little coaxing from the peanut gallery, that that would be a good name for the dog, whose paws were already huge, hinting he was destined to grow into his name.

Together, Matt and Jeff made supper and, after cleaning up, ran a bath for Mikey. The puppy - a Labrador Retriever, a breed known for their love of the water – decided it would be fun to join Mikey, his new best buddy, in the tub. It took all four of Matt and Jeff's hands to separate the two, with it a draw as to which was wetter, the puppy or Mikey.

That was actually easier than the next problem. When they tried to put Mikey to bed, he wanted the puppy to go to bed with him, and the puppy had the same idea. But Jeff thought the puppy should sleep in the temporary doggy bed he'd set up for him in the living room.

In the end, after tears and whines from Mikey and the puppy, it proved impossible to separate the two, and Jeff caved, thinking he'd try again the next day. But it was a hopeless cause,

Thomas Willard © 2023

and the two ended up sharing the bed until Mikey, then Mike, left for college 14 years later.

After they, really Jeff, relented and let the puppy sleep with Mikey, the house grew quiet. A half-hour after the commotion had ended, Matt and Jeff checked Mikey's room and found the two curled up together, fast asleep.

As they were returning to the living room, Jeff had a change of mind and asked Matt to lie down with him in his bedroom: his leg was bothering him, and he asked Matt if he'd give it a massage. Matt, concerned Jeff was in pain, said sure.

Once in the bedroom, Jeff, on crutches, asked Matt to help him off with his clothes. Again, Matt said sure. But then Jeff began undressing Matt.

Matt, not wanting to start something he couldn't finish, balked, and asked,

"Why do I have to get undressed?"

Jeff, knowing Matt would catch on sooner rather than later, tried to slough off Matt's concerns by giving his standard answer,

Thomas Willard © 2023

"I just want to keep things even."

But when Matt stopped undressing him, Jeff decided it was time to come clean.

"I need to talk with you, Matt, about something very important. And I need to trust what you tell me. The only way I'll believe you is if we're naked, pressed together, face-to-face."

Seeing the anguish in Jeff's eyes, Matt resumed undressing Jeff and let Jeff undress him.

When they were both naked, Matt helped Jeff into bed and then crawled in after him. They turned to face each other before Jeff put an arm around Matt and drew him in until they were pressed together.

Both Matt and Jeff's bodies instantly reacted to the intimate contact, though Matt initially tried to reduce the groin-to-groin contact pressure.

Jeff waited until Matt gave up on trying to minimize their groin contact and relax. When he felt Matt go with the flow and start to breathe normally, Jeff knew he was past Matt's defenses and could trust whatever Matt told him from then on.

"Matt, my leg is fine. I'm sorry for trying to trick you into lying with me like this, but I'm desperate and at my wits' end.

"I need your help. You're the only one that can help me. But by asking for your help, I'm putting pressure on you, and I don't want to do that; it's not fair. That's why I didn't ask you before."

Matt could see tears begin flowing from Jeff's eyes, so Matt reached over to stroke Jeff's hair to comfort him, but Jeff stopped him.

"No, I don't need that kind of help from you. I need you to be honest, to tell me the truth about what you want, what you need.

"I know what I need and want. Last night it became really clear to Linda and me.

"Your plan yesterday worked, and I was able to make love to Linda, just like before Korea.

Thomas Willard © 2023

"But when I tried a second time a half hour later without your help, I failed.

"Linda was great and jumped right in to reassure me and told me not to worry, that everything would be fine.

"But she and I both knew I wasn't going to be fine unless I figured out what was bothering me.

"I drew a blank, so Linda told me what she thought it was, and I think she's absolutely right.

"I need to be emotionally and physically intimate with you, and it's not ever going away. My body waited patiently for years for me to figure a way to be with you, but it's given up on me, and it's now demanding a change, or it won't let me get aroused with anyone except you, not even with myself.

"I've tried to tell you before how much you mean to me, and I can understand why you don't quite believe me because I also love and desire Linda.

"But my body doesn't lie. Check me out right now; you can feel me; I'm hard as nails, leaking like a sieve, just lying next to you."

Matt had never seen Jeff upset like this. He was aching to help him in any way, but Jeff wouldn't let him touch him to try and soothe or console him.

Matt, also crying a little, said, "Jeff, I'll do anything you want. Just tell me what to do. I don't know what you want or need."

"Matt, you're the best planner I've ever met. Way better than me, especially in the air.

"But when it comes to plans that involve me and our relationship, your plans are terrible.

"You mean well, always want what's best for me, and you're always trying your best to do the honorable thing.

"But you care so much for me that you're blind and can't see straight. You don't have this problem with anyone else.

Thomas Willard © 2023

"I think you're like Superman, and I'm your Kryptonite, destroying your normally superior powers of perception and reason.

"I need you to tell me what you want and not to worry about what's the right and honorable thing to do; to be selfish this once and tell me what you want.

"You're too ready to sacrifice your own happiness for what you think is mine – not realizing that your happiness and mine are the same things - that you've confused me, and I'm no longer sure.

"I used to be certain you wanted me emotionally and physically, but you went years without touching me intimately or letting me touch you that way.

"You gave me some hope that one time in the showers at Langley. But you were so remorseful afterward that I could never bring myself to mention it.

"You know me, I always have a plan. I have one I've been sitting on since before I got married, but I screwed up one detail and never got to put it into action.

Thomas Willard © 2023

"I'm afraid to tell you about it now because you're too nice and will agree to anything just to make me feel better. But it's my best plan ever, better than my scheme to seduce you at the flak house in Romsey. But you have to tell me what you really want this one time, or I won't share it. If you do, I promise I'll trust you forever and will never ask you again."

Matt, never good at knowing his emotions, dug deep. If he told Jeff what he really wanted, it could end his marriage. But if he didn't say anything, Jeff could be left in misery for the rest of his life. So, Matt, now openly sobbing, told Jeff just that.

"I'm afraid to tell you what I want and need because it could affect your marriage. I don't want that. I couldn't handle that!"

Jeff, sensing they were on the verge of a breakthrough, encouraged Matt.

"Matt, I'm asking you to trust me. I know you're horrible with our relationship stuff; you mean well, but your plans suck. If you just tell me the truth this one time, once I know what you really want, I promise I'll handle everything from here on out, and you'll like how things turn out for everyone.

"I've never wanted to dominate you, even though I think you might have let me. I didn't want that for you. That's the real reason I've insisted on keeping things even. You probably noticed my promise in Romsey not to keep things even anymore only lasted about two weeks.

"But this is different. You have a distorted view of yourself and don't see yourself the way I see you, as the finest person in the world. That's why I need to take control of our relationship. You can take control of everything else to even things out."

Then Jeff said, "Come closer. Look at your reflection in my eyes; I can see mine in yours. That's how I see you, how I want you to see yourself from now on."

Matt, shivering, now much more upset than Jeff, in a quivering voice said,

"I need you, and I've always wanted you. If I've ever led you to believe otherwise, it was just an act. When I jumped your bones in the barracks' showers, that showed how I really feel about you."

Jeff stopped crying and kissed and held an obviously distraught Matt until he calmed down a little, then gently said,

"Thank you for telling me, Matt. I know that was hard, but I needed you to say that.

"I should have told you before, but I lost your medallion in Japan. Hopefully, this will make up for it a little."

Jeff then reached into the nightstand's drawer and pulled out a small bundle. Wrapped in a handkerchief were two nearly identical 1947-class "Brass Rat" MIT graduate rings, one engraved with Matt's name and the other with Jeff's.

Then Jeff began the vow he'd rehearsed in his head a thousand times since graduation.

"Matt, I planned to do this before I got married, but it took longer to buy the rings than I thought.

"You remember when I got measured for my wedding ring, and I playfully had the jeweler measure your fingers, too? Well,

Thomas Willard © 2023

this is why. I guessed we were the same size – we are - but I needed to be sure before I ordered these," as Jeff unwrapped the bundle and held out the two rings in his hand for Matt to see. Jeff took Matt's right hand, then continued in a sincere, somber voice,

"I need you to know you are the most important person in my life and that I will always be there for you, your "Forever Wingman." And I mean forever. I intend to be buried with you in a shared grave in Arlington National Cemetery – we both received the Silver Star, so are eligible for a below-ground burial there - with both of us wearing these rings," as Jeff placed his ring on Matt's ring finger. Then he handed the ring engraved with Matt's name to Matt and said, "Your turn."

Matt took the ring and Jeff's right hand and, with tears pouring down his face, in a barely audible voice, managed to get out, "I promise to be your "Forever Wingman," too," placing the ring on Jeff's ring finger before they kissed and hugged each other. Then he added, "And you didn't lose my medallion. It vanished into thin air when it used all its magic up helping to save your leg."

Thomas Willard © 2023

Jeff said, "I guess I should have let you know before, but this ring means you own me, all of me. You can share me with Linda, hopefully, but that's up to you."

Then pointing at the graduation ring on his finger, Jeff said, "This ring trumps that one," pointing at his wedding ring, then added, "at least according to Linda."

Jeff continued, "And Linda says no more hiding our affection for each other from her. You're going to have to get used to her seeing us holding and being intimate with each other. She even wants us to shower together like we used to in Swampscott. We'll still need to be discrete around Mikey, but not once he's in bed, not when it's just Linda and us."

"You're getting the room next to ours, the one with a connecting door.

"And I want to go back to sharing clothes with you, living out of the same dresser and closet. I loved wearing your clothes and seeing you wearing mine. I want them jumbled up so we don't know whose is whose anymore. To be honest, back in Swampscott,

I used to steal your dirty laundry and wear them the next day just to smell you a little, to feel closer to you.

Matt, lightening a little, said, "I used to steal your dirty clothes, too, for the same reason, so we're even."

Then he jokingly added, "I guess this means you own all of me, too. You're not going to rent me out or anything, are you?"

Jeff, smiling, said, "No, but I have other plans for you. Well, your, I guess now, my swimmers. I want you to be a sperm donor for Linda and me. Seriously, though, would you consider doing that? I know it's a lot to ask."

Matt, now also smiling, said, "Hey, you own me now, there's no need to ask permission, what's mine is yours. But first, I think I'm going to help you make a little donation of your own," as Matt reached for Jeff's penis.

After they'd each enjoyed an orgasm at the other's hand, Jeff solemnly said,

"I'm going to let your dad know about the lifelong commitment we've just made to each other and that he doesn't

Thomas Willard © 2023

need to worry about you being left on your own anymore; I'll always be there for you, and he can relax, you're my responsibility now. If he's ever worried that our relationship might have changed, he only needs to see the rings on our fingers to know that it hasn't.

"I consider myself part of your family, and you, part of both of mine – the one in Oak Park and the one here in Concord - at least as much as any in-law is, and your dad as my dad, too. But that's not new; I've always felt that way about him. I'm going to ask him if he'll let me call him Dad. I can't tell you how many times I've almost accidentally called him Dad since first meeting him."

Then, holding Matt's hand and feeling his ring, Jeff added,

"My happiness starts and ends with you. You have no idea how happy you've just made me by agreeing to wear this ring and promising to be my "Forever Wingman," then, emphasizing the end of a sore point, added, "and that means no backsliding, ever again!" as a single tear ran down his cheek, getting, "I promise,"

Thomas Willard © 2023

and a soft kiss on the lips from an equally teary-eyed Matt in response.

Jeff felt a pang of guilt for not letting Matt know there was a second half to his and Linda's plan. But he was certain now he was working in Matt's best interest and resolved that going forward, he'd make all the tough, moral calls for them both in their relationship, subject to Frank's approval of the second half of their wildly unconventional – Jeff worried Frank might say immoral - plan. Jeff thought, "Next stop, Swampscott."

#

THREE-WAY BLESSING

When Linda returned home from work at a little past midnight early on Friday morning, she found Matt asleep in Linda and Jeff's bed, with Jeff lying next to him, rubbing his back.

While he slept, Jeff had partially dressed Matt, putting him in his boxers and t-shirt before Jeff put on his underwear. He knew Matt would have been mortified if Linda found them in her bed, naked. But that was exactly where Linda and Jeff wanted things headed; they just needed to gently ease Matt into joining their physical relationship. The first step was for the three of them to share a bed for a night, partially clothed, just sleeping.

Matt slept through until 6:00 am the following morning. When he awoke, he found himself in bed with a still-sleeping Jeff and Linda, with Jeff in the middle, Matt's front pressed against Jeff's back, and with his arm around Jeff. Though embarrassed, Matt didn't freak out but quietly got up to check on Mikey. Before leaving the bedroom, he glanced back at Jeff, holding Linda from behind, and thought about how peaceful they both looked.

Around 8:30 am, partially lured by the smell of fresh coffee brewing and bacon and eggs cooking, Linda and Jeff got up and joined Matt in the kitchen for breakfast.

By then, Mikey and Moose, having been fed earlier, and spending two hours roughhousing with each other, were ready for a nap. Matt carried them separately to the nearby couch in the

Thomas Willard © 2023

living room, covered them with a blanket, and then rejoined Linda and Jeff in the kitchen.

As Matt passed Linda, seated at the kitchen table, she stopped him and asked him to show her his ring.

Matt, blushing profusely but proud of his ring, placed his right hand in Linda's so she could get a closer look. Linda, looking into Matt's eyes in a sincere, gentle voice, said,

"It's a beautiful ring. And I know the love and commitment that it represents. I'm so happy for you both; you have no idea," then she kissed him on the cheek before leaning across the table to kiss Jeff's cheek, too.

Jeff told Matt he was going to call Frank to let him know about the commitment they'd made to each other as soon as possible so that Frank wouldn't be worried as much about Matt anymore.

Jeff called Frank that evening and asked if they could visit him in Swampscott the next day, Saturday, around noon. He told Frank not to be concerned, the news was good, and that he thought he had a solution to his, Matt's, and Linda's relationship problem but wanted to run it by Frank first before discussing it with Matt.

Frank said they were welcome to stop by; he'd make them lunch. He had a reservation with the vet to take the puppy in for his shots at 3:00 pm, but he could cancel it if Jeff thought they'd need more time to discuss the problem.

Jeff said he didn't want Frank to go to the trouble of making them lunch; they'd stop along the way and pick up submarine sandwiches for everyone to eat at Frank's house. And he thought he'd only need about a half hour of Frank's time.

Frank and his new puppy, Bear – a name chosen by Mikey to go with Moose - were on the front porch waiting when Matt pulled into the driveway at noon. Mikey, quickly followed by Moose, poured out of the car first and raced for Frank to hug him. The puppies, recognizing each other by smell, instantly started barking and roughhousing together, quickly joined by Mikey.

Frank greeted Linda, Jeff, and Matt, each with a hug, and then followed them into the house.

They ate lunch at the kitchen table, with Mikey sneaking pieces of cold cuts to the puppies. Then after they'd cleaned up, Jeff asked Frank if they could all go for a walk along the beach.

It being February, the beach was deserted. And Jeff, on crutches, held back with Frank while Linda and Matt chased after Mikey and the puppies a little distance ahead.

Jeff started by telling Frank about the lifelong commitment he and Matt had made to each other, symbolized by their wearing each other's MIT graduation rings.

Then he told Frank about the plan for him and Matt to be buried together in a shared grave at Arlington. He said the idea had begun with his conviction that Matt, being an Ace in two wars, having received a Silver Star for heroism, and having declined The Congressional Medal of Honor – not to mention the countless bomber crew lives he'd saved - deserved to be buried there. But he thought Matt wouldn't think he deserved the honor. Then Jeff thought Matt would agree if Jeff were buried there, too. Alington's shortage of space, and Jeff's desire to be buried as close to Matt as possible, led to the shared-grave idea.

Jeff thought the decision of where to be buried was only about bringing comfort to the deceased and their family. Linda wanted to be buried with her parents in a family plot in Lowell, but Lowell meant nothing to Jeff, and the thought of being buried there was a little unsettling.

There was no Sullivan family plot in Oak Park, but there were so many Sullivans in the area that they practically took over half of the local cemetery. If Jeff was buried in Oak Park, though, he'd just join the rest of the Sullivan clan buried there.

Jeff knew that Frank wanted to be buried next to his wife in Peabody but wasn't sure if he intended Matt to be buried there as well. So, Jeff asked Frank how he felt about Matt being buried at Arlington with Jeff and the lifelong Wingman commitment they'd made to each other.

Frank was stunned by what Jeff had just told him. All the thought Jeff had put into coming up with the commitment, the love that it represented, left Frank so choked up he could initially only respond by wrapping his arms around Jeff, pulling him into a tight embrace.

After a few minutes, fighting threw his emotions, Frank tried to speak.

"Jeff, I'm always amazed by how considerate, perceptive, and thoughtful you are; it shows how deeply you love Matt. But this time, what you've come up with is off the charts and is probably the most romantic, loving arrangement I've ever heard of, making the standard wedding vows pale in comparison.

"As far as the lifelong commitment vow you've exchanged with Matt, I couldn't be happier, and the rings provide the tangible proof of your love that Matt needs to help prevent his backsliding. But I'm not half the romantic you are and would never have thought of it.

"As far as where Matt will be buried goes, it's hard for a parent to think about the death of their child. So I haven't made any arrangements for Matt; there is no adjacent plot for him next to Kathryn's and mine in Peabody.

"Again, your idea of the two of you sharing a grave at Arlington has left me stunned, but already it's bringing me comfort knowing he'll be honored there and buried in the same grave as the love of his life.

"By the way, you deserve to be buried there just as much as Matt – you've earned all the same honors, or you wouldn't be eligible.

"You keep telling me how much smarter Matt is than you and how much better he is at certain things than you.

"But you couldn't be more wrong. You're just as smart as Matt, more like each other than either of you know. You complement each other and bootstrap each other up if one is stronger in an area than the other. That's how you became such an excellent sailor and swimmer, and Matt a great cook and dancer. I'm waiting for you to teach Matt about business – I've noticed that you are pretty savvy at it – and for Matt to show you how to

Thomas Willard © 2023

play the piano. Together, I think you two can do anything, and that's no exaggeration."

Then Jeff, red-faced, said,

"You and Matt are part of my family, and I've always felt I was part of yours.

"I rarely get to see my dad, and Linda's parents are a little older, and though they love me, they are not aware of the depth of my and Matt's relationship, so I'm not as close to them as I am to you.

"Would you mind if I call you Dad? I feel like, in a way, Matt and I are married to each other, and if we were, I'd get to call you Dad."

Frank pulled Jeff in for another hug, then said, "I'd be honored if you called me Dad. I think you may have slipped up a couple of times already and called me Dad by accident. But I'm not replacing your dad, who I like a lot. I'll just be his stand-in when he's not near, OK?"

Thomas Willard © 2023

Jeff said, "Thank you. But you may change your mind in a few minutes. Matt and me making our lifelong commitment vows to each other was the first and most important step in sorting out the tangled relationship between Matt, Linda, and me.

"You may kick me out of your family when I tell you about the second half of the solution. I haven't shared it with Matt and won't unless you approve. But it wasn't something Linda and I thought we could discuss with Matt: we knew he'd bolt for the door, blushing profusely, two seconds after we started talking about the solution we'd come up with to our tangled relationship problem. But we think we can seduce him as I did at the flak house in Romsey, and he'll be fine twenty minutes later. We won't try to seduce him, though, unless you approve of our unconventional solution."

Jeff began by telling Frank of his two intimate sexual problems: that besides his leg injury, the fine tubing in his testicles had been injured during ejection and resulted in a low sperm count, so low that he was considered sterile; and that since returning from

Korea, he'd been unable to perform with Linda and thought he was impotent.

Matt's intervention the day after their visit to Mass General proved that Jeff wasn't impotent, as did the sex-ambush Matt arranged for Jeff with Linda the next day. But when he failed during the second round with her that day, Linda correctly diagnosed the problem: Jeff's body was insisting on intimate contact with Matt and would hold Jeff's manhood hostage until he made it happen, with the first step being entering into a lifelong commitment with Matt, something Jeff had planned for and always intended to do.

Then Linda shocked Jeff with the solution to two of their other problems. She no longer cared about having another baby, but if Jeff was going to leave her because he was sterile, maybe they could ask Matt to be a natural sperm donor.

Jeff said he thought Matt would agree to be a donor until he learned the details of what being a natural sperm donor involved; then, his shyness and honor code would prevent him from doing it.

Thomas Willard © 2023

That's when Linda shocked Jeff even more by suggesting they have a three-way sexual relationship with Matt: they were already in a three-way relationship, but because of Matt, it wasn't sexual. She didn't want Matt and Jeff to hide their affection or intimate sexual acts from her anymore. And if Matt was going to be a natural donor, he was going to see a lot of what Jeff and Linda got up to in bed, too, and would need Jeff's help to make his donations. Then Linda admitted that since Matt's help with Jeff's medical issue, she'd developed a crush on Matt, become very curious about his body, and was now excited about having his baby.

Jeff said he liked Linda's plan, wasn't shocked by it, just grateful, and thought she was a genius, as good as Spiegel. But then reality set in, and Jeff said Matt would never get on board; he was too honorable for his own good and too shy to boot.

So, Linda suggested they get Frank to approve both Matt being a donor and Linda and Jeff's plan to lure Matt into a three-way sexual relationship. If Frank approved, they'd use whatever devious methods necessary to get Matt in bed.

When Jeff finished briefing Frank on the plan, he said,

"I know we're asking Matt to join an extremely unconventional relationship, one you may think is immoral and not approve of. But when I think of the benefits, that Matt will have a chance to become a father – I won't care about being sterile if Matt's my stand-in - Linda will have a chance to have another baby - maybe even a girl, that you may become a granddad, and that I'll be in an intimate relationship with the two people I love the most, not to mention that both Matt and you will belong to my and Linda's family, especially if there's a baby, I can't see anything wrong with the idea. We just have to be flexible and make our own rules."

After absorbing all the details, an astonished Frank said,

"This is a perfect solution. I wouldn't tweak it in any way. I approve of your solution, but you don't need my approval; Matt's already told you that you own him. I'd go with that."

Thomas Willard © 2023

Jeff asked, a little concerned, "What about Spiegel's rule to always be honest and open?"

Frank, still a little miffed at Spiegel for what he put Matt through to help Jeff, said,

"Spiegel is the most dishonest and manipulative person I know and doesn't follow his own advice. You should ignore him on this one."

Then Jeff, already feeling guilty for what Frank was permitting him to subject Matt to, asked, "Do you think this will be too much for Matt? My seduction plan at the flak house in Romsey only involved some close body contact while dancing."

Frank, seeing the concern on Jeff's face, said, "I trust you completely with Matt.

"You should take a page from your brothers' playbook and crash through Matt's personal space. Just don't draw things out; it will give him too much time to build his fears sky-high. Your over-and-done-in-twenty-minutes seems like a good time frame. And always have some part of you in contact with him to reassure him."

Thomas Willard © 2023

Frank asked when they were planning to seduce Matt. Jeff said they were waiting for Frank's approval, so they hadn't made any arrangements yet, but it would be soon. Whenever it was, they'd drop Mikey off at the sitter's first.

Then Frank said, "Why not today, right now? I'm getting ready to take Bear to the vet for a checkup and some shots. I could take Mikey and Moose with me and ask the vet to give Moose a checkup and his shots, too. We'd be gone for at least a couple of hours, and you could use my bedroom: Matt's bed is probably too small for the three of you."

Jeff waved to Linda, signaling her to join him and Frank, leaving Matt, Mikey, and the puppies still out of earshot.

When she arrived and was standing next to Jeff, Frank told her he approved all parts of their plan, including Matt being a sperm donor and Linda and Jeff's plan to seduce him into joining a three-way romantic relationship. Then he said,

"Linda, I always knew you were the key to finding a solution, but I hadn't a clue as to what a solution would look like.

"The solution you've come up with – a three-way intimate relationship, with Matt as a donor - is brilliant and solves all your problems; all but one, that is, getting Matt to go along. But your seduction plan should work, too, if you don't give Matt time to think, at least not until you get him in bed, naked.

"I told Jeff I'm getting ready to go the vet's now, and I can take Mikey and Moose with me. You're welcome to seduce Matt here, now, before you and Jeff have a chance to get cold feet. We should be gone at least two hours, and you're welcome to use my bedroom."

Then Frank added, "I guess I've joined your seduction conspiracy. I know I can trust you two, that you always have Matt's best interests in mind. But I admit I may not be the most objective person anymore, knowing there's a chance I could become a grandfather."

Frank waved to Matt, signaling he, Mikey, and the puppies should join him while Linda and Jeff huddled. Then Linda left Jeff and went into the house.

Thomas Willard © 2023

When Matt arrived, Jeff, in an excited voice, said, "Linda says it's time; we need to get you ready to donate now."

Then Frank said, "Matt, I'm going to take Mikey and both puppies to the vet with me. We should be gone for at least a couple of hours. Jeff, could you get Mikey and the dogs ready and put them in the car? I want to speak with Matt for a second."

When Jeff was out of earshot, Frank said,

"Jeff's gone over the lifelong commitment arrangement he's made with you, what your rings symbolize, and I couldn't be happier. Even his plans for you and him to be buried at Arlington. It's perfect, something only Jeff could come up with, and it shows just how much he loves you. He's an incredible guy.

"He also told me you've agreed to be a sperm donor for him and Linda and that I might become a granddad. The thought of getting to hold your baby," as Frank paused to gain control of his emotions, "is overwhelming."

Then, in a gentle, supportive voice, he said,

"You're smart and clever enough to know there's more coming. I'm not going to spoil all of Linda and Jeff's scheming efforts by giving you any details. Just know they asked for my approval of the next part of their plan, and I gladly gave it.

"Their happiness and yours now rests on only two things; your ability to face your fears, and with Jeff's help, I know you will, and for you to abandon your rigid honor code for a flexible set of rules that Linda, Jeff, and you come up with on your own.

"You three are the most honorable people that I know and don't need to adhere to a rigid set of rules, some written by those who used to hang people they thought were different – people they labeled as witches - in Salem, a twenty-minute drive from here. Their kind today would imprison you and Jeff, give you forced frontal lobotomies or electric shock treatments, and even chemically or surgically castrate you just for loving one another. There are even some zealots who would think they'd be justified in severely beating or killing you both.

Thomas Willard © 2023

"I should have spoken to you before when you were fighting against your emerging feelings in high school. I made a big mistake then in giving you your privacy, leaving you to sort things out on your own. Spiegel set me straight, though, telling me to always be direct and honest with you, and I'm never going to make that mistake again.

"You have low self-esteem because you think you're different. But you can't pick and choose only the parts of yourself you consider as appropriate. Your character is made of the sum of your parts; it's a package deal. You can't cut any part of your personality out without affecting the rest of you.

"To me, you're perfect just the way you are and always have been. Except for the anguish you've suffered quietly on your own, I wouldn't change a thing and couldn't be more proud of you.

"And if that's not enough for you to feel better about yourself, consider this. Your character, all of it, is why Jeff is here today, just like his character is the reason you're here.

Thomas Willard © 2023

"You're going to have to choose now between your honor code – a code you didn't get from me, I hope – and your love for Jeff. Keep only the good parts of your code – the parts that Jeff agrees are good – and dump the rest into the ocean."

Matt, shivering - Frank had never spoken to him like that before - hugged his dad and said,

"I love you, Dad. I know you're giving me your best advice. I'll do what you say, and from now on, only go by Jeff's honor system. I know mine's flawed because it would label Jeff a deviant just for loving me. As far as I'm concerned, the ocean can have the whole code; together, we'll come up with our own set of rules from scratch."

Frank, now even more proud of Matt, said,

"There's one more thing. Jeff is an extremely honorable man. He's still haunted by your first time together when he thinks he might have forced himself on you after you said no. You saved him by showing him that you loved and wanted him just as much, but it came close.

Thomas Willard © 2023

"You may soon find yourself in a similar position, where you are being pushed into a situation you find extremely uncomfortable. You can say anything you want to protest, even try to resist or escape, but whatever you do, be very careful about saying no.

"If you do, you could tear Jeff apart. For Jeff, it would be like giving someone he loves medicine they don't want. What should Jeff do if the person says no; force it on him anyway, knowing it's for his own good, or should he respect the wishes of the one he loves and risk his dying from the illness?"

With resolve, Matt said,

"I promise, Dad, no matter what he does to me, I won't say no to Jeff.

"When I said no before, I wasn't speaking to him; I was speaking to myself, trying to stop from shaming myself.

"As soon as I get a chance, the next time I get him alone, I'll let Jeff know I wasn't speaking to him when I said no in

Romsey and that he's never forced himself on me. I'm the one that forced myself on him in the showers at Langley."

Then Frank, in a much lighter mood, said, as he mussed Matt's hair,

"That's good. You have a lot of courage; I'm so very proud of you.

"I wouldn't feel bad about Langley. Jeff told me that after two years of your not being willing to be with him, Langley gave him hope that you still wanted him physically. And besides that, he always thinks it's cute when you instigate things and are aggressive with him.

"I know how good of an actor you can be; you fool me all the time. Just go with the flow and act surprised, indignant, and embarrassed. Linda and Jeff have put a lot of thought into their seduction plan. Give them a break and let them have a little fun for a chance; they've earned it," getting a big smooch from Matt on the cheek.

#

Thomas Willard © 2023

SEDUCTION

Once Frank had pulled out of the driveway, Jeff immediately started seducing Matt, saying he had to get him ready for his sperm donation, which according to Linda's body signs, needed to happen today as soon as possible.

Jeff brought Matt upstairs to the bathroom, shut the door, and began undressing Matt and himself, saying he was going to take a shower with Matt to get him nice and clean. Matt continued undressing, and when they were both naked, they climbed into the shower together.

Jeff thoroughly soaped and scrubbed Matt's back and front, then rinsed him and began shampooing his hair. Just when Matt was blinded by the shampoo, there was a knock on the door, and Linda entered, asking why it was taking them so long. Jeff, pretending he couldn't hear her over the running water, opened the shower curtain, exposing Matt. Matt, who still couldn't see, felt that he was being exposed to Linda and tried to cover up, not sure which way to turn.

Jeff placed his hands on Matt's shoulders and turned him towards Linda while rinsing the soap from Matt's hair. As soon as Matt's eyes were free of soap, he opened them and was mortified to find Linda staring right at him and his half-hard erection.

Covering his groin as best he could with his hands, he turned towards Jeff, which gave Linda an unobstructed view of his back and butt. Matt, now totally embarrassed and unable to speak, let out a whimpered, "Oh!"

Linda said, "Come on guys, stop stalling; it's time. My temperature is perfect," before leaving the bathroom and closing the door behind her.

Jeff said, "Yes, we need to get a move on. Linda's always pretty scientific about this pregnancy stuff and knows when it's the best time."

Matt, still shocked at being exposed and laboring under the impression he was going to provide a donation in a test tube or

Thomas Willard © 2023

Petrie dish, was confused. When were they going to go to the doctor's office or hospital, and why did he have to be so clean?

He let Jeff dry him, then wrapped a towel around his waist before leading him, he thought, to his bedroom to get dressed.

But Jeff led him instead to Frank's bedroom, where they found Linda in bed, under the covers.

Matt asked, "Why are we in here, and why is Linda in bed? I thought we had to leave soon."

Jeff said, "No, we don't have to go anywhere. You're going to make your donation here."

Matt, now totally confused and mortified, blushing profusely, said, "Then why does Linda have to be here to watch?"

Jeff, realizing his ruse had gone as far as it could, said,

"Linda has to be here. You're going to deposit your sperm donation in her," as he gently removed the towel around Matt's waist.

Matt let out a yelp and tried to cover up. But Jeff let his towel drop and said, "See, we're even now," as he pulled the

Thomas Willard © 2023

covers back and gently guided Matt, who was covering his groin with his hands as best he could, to kneel on the bed to the side of Linda.

Jeff hugged Matt, who was shivering from fright, for a few moments before starting his explanation.

"Matt, I know I was deceptive and vague about the details when I asked you to be a sperm donor. But if I'd told you what we had in mind – yes, Linda's part of this scheme, she's going to let me explain it to you – you're so shy and have this rigid honor code, you'd never have agreed.

"I knew the only hope for this plan to work was to get you naked and expose you to Linda first. We've done that already; the hard part's over. Linda's much prettier than Mrs. Frobisher, can bake just as good an apple pie, and you love her, so your embarrassment should be much less.

"But before we did that, I asked your dad for his approval, not just for you to be a donor, but for you to be part of a three-way physical relationship with Linda and me, with me at the center.

Thomas Willard © 2023

You've already been part of a three-way relationship for more than five years; it just hasn't been physical because your honor code wouldn't allow it.

"So, you see, this is more than about you being a donor and the three of us having a baby together. Linda and I want you to join us in a romantic relationship and for the three of us to have sex together.

"Before you get too freaked out, we both know you're not into women sexually; we're not trying to change you. But we do want you to be a sperm donor and, hopefully, become a father and make your dad a granddad. Linda would get to have another baby, and I'd be thrilled if you became a father.

"The safest, most certain, and least expensive way is to be a donor the natural way. The other way, artificial insemination, involves a risky medical procedure for the woman and is not perfected yet: the success rate is very low. I know I led you to believe that that is what we were asking of you, but it was never really an option that we considered.

Thomas Willard © 2023

"I told you the other day I have a physical need to be with you. My body insists on it and has me on a very short leash – a six-inch long leash. You promised we could resume being intimate together, which gave my body hope, and I have been hard nearly every minute since, which is starting to concern me some, thinking maybe I'll damage myself. I'd much rather have that problem to worry about, though, than the other.

"But if you were to change your mind, I'd have to divorce Linda – I've already told her I couldn't stay with her being both sterile and impotent.

"If we do resume having sex together- there, I've admitted it in front of Linda, that we have sex together – then how do we manage it without sneaking around or leaving Linda feeling excluded?

"I was at a total loss when Linda came up with the perfect solution: Why can't the three of us have sex together? She loves it when she catches us being affectionate with one another and has always been curious about what we get up to. I'm not ashamed of

Thomas Willard © 2023

any of it, and I don't think you should be, either. She admits she'd find it a little erotic watching us, though she'd try to give us some privacy, especially if we're having flashbacks and need to hold each other and cry it out. She knows we haven't dealt with the Korean rescue mission yet.

"And you'd be there when I make love to Linda. You'd see how different it is than when I make love to you. The way we kiss, hold each other and touch, it's all different. When I'm with you, we're like the same species; we know what the other is feeling, and there is mutual feedback between us that builds to a simultaneous climax. When I feel you in my hands, I almost feel like I'm reading your mind and you mine.

"With Linda, it's more like a different species. We're built differently, so the feedback isn't as strong, and I can only tell what she's feeling by what she says and does. The natural plug-and-socket anatomy, though, results in a rhythm that feels primal, with more grunting and thrusting with Linda than with you. It's hard to explain, but if you watched us together, you'd get a better sense of what I mean.

"As far as your donating sperm the natural way goes, I'll be there to guide you, literally: the only hands on your groin, at least initially, will be mine. I'll get you worked up first as you did to me the other day for my sex ambush, and I'll use my secret technique – well, maybe not so secret – to get you to thrust and build to a climax for both you and Linda.

"I have to be honest, Matt; I must be a pervert because this talk is making me hard as nails. And Linda confessed that by the way you handled my medical issue – giving her a brief glimpse of the decisive, fearless Matt that I know - she's developed a crush on you and is very curious about your body.

"If you go along with this, Matt, you'll make me the happiest and the horniest guy in the world. I think I could more than satisfy you and Linda sexually. And Linda would be happy, too, being made love to by two men who she thinks are the world's

Thomas Willard © 2023

sexiest studs, and hopefully having a baby - maybe a girl, but she won't care either way - with you, too.

"I know having a baby is a serious responsibility. Again, I spoke with your dad and told him that Linda and I had considered as many contingencies as we could think of. Your dad approved our plans, and I hope you do, too.

"If anything were to happen to me, I'd want you to marry Linda and adopt all the children. If anything were to happen to you, Linda and I would raise yours and my children as our own, but we would let the children you fathered know, as soon as they were old enough to understand, that you were their biological dad, and that your dad was their grandfather. And if anything were to happen to Linda, I'd never marry again, and you and I would raise the children together."

Looking into Matt's eyes, Jeff said,

"I know this is extremely unconventional. But I tried to come up with a more conventional plan to be with you and Linda, and I failed. Your plans are always the same and involve your leaving me, thinking I'd be better off without you. You couldn't be more wrong; I'd be miserable for the rest of my life if you left me or if anything were to happen to you.

Linda came up with the seeds of this plan once she figured out why my body was failing me. She was worried I'd be shocked by her plan, but I couldn't be more grateful and relieved. I think she's a genius and could give Spiegel a run for his money.

"I know you probably have trouble speaking now. Maybe you need more time to think about things. But I think you'd be happy if you joined Linda and me if you could just throw away your rigid honor code - a code that wasn't written for us - and follow Spiegel's advice and come up with our own set of rules."

Jeff, still holding Matt, whose shivering had stopped, could feel they were both fully erect, though because their bodies were still pressed together, Linda couldn't see them.

Not knowing what Matt was thinking, Jeff gambled and, in a tender and encouraging voice, said,

"It's a lot to lay on you all at once. I won't try to convince you anymore now. Maybe we can get together in Concord in a few days after you've had a chance to think things over. But if you've already decided, one way or another, I think you know what to do next."

Matt knew that by reaching for the towel to cover himself up and then leaving for his bedroom, as his naturally shy nature was screaming for him to do, Jeff would assume he had decided not to join their relationship. So instead, Matt did the exact opposite. He broke from his embrace with Jeff, then moved to the side into the clear, fully exposing himself to Linda.

Jeff was at first beside himself with joy but then gained control of himself and asked,

"Matt, are you sure? I've put a lot of pressure on you the past few days. We don't need to do this now."

Matt nodded yes, kissed Linda, then Jeff, before managing to haltingly say,

"I'm – yours, you – own – me," displaying his ring to Jeff.

Thomas Willard © 2023

Linda, having sat upright for most of Jeff's explanation but still covered by her sheets, knelt on her knees in front of Matt, then let her sheets fall to the side, exposing herself to Matt, saying, "I'm just like Jeff and like to keep things even," then added, "You're beautiful, Matt, just as I imagined you were. You and Jeff have nearly the same body; it's amazing! I'm so lucky."

Then Jeff said, "I know Linda and me have been pretty conniving and devious trying to lure you into this relationship. But it's hard to talk to you about things like this, and we didn't know what else to do.

"But from now on, the three of us are going to be open and honest with each other. We'll be equal partners, and there'll be no two-against-one plotting or talking about one of us behind their back, though I expect you and Linda will bond when comparing notes about me while I'm taking my usual 20-minute nap after having sex. My ears may be burning as I wake up, but I won't mind a bit.

Thomas Willard © 2023

"Linda's pretty perceptive, and she's going to call you out if she senses you're starting to backslide. She's noticed that you and I give off early warning signs that we're not getting enough physical, intimate time with each other.

"My warning sign, which appears after about two days of not being with you, is I wake up without a morning erection, which can quickly lead to complete impotency if you and I don't get together soon afterward.

"Your warning sign, probably also appearing two days after being separated from me, is you start to drift, becoming less open to physical contact, and you keep yourself separated from me by at least six feet. That's when you begin planning your escape, thinking I'd be better off without you, creating a positive feedback loop, when you can quickly spiral out of control.

"The solution is easy: more physical contact – sex – between us. But it's easy for me to miss the clues. Now that we have Linda watching for the signs, too, I don't think we'll have as much of a problem.

Thomas Willard © 2023

"I want you to speak up and tell us how you're feeling, though, if anything's upsetting you and if you think you're starting to backslide. But I know it's hard for you to always know your feelings.

"I'm not going to mess around. If Linda or I notice you drifting, or Linda notices I'm showing the first signs of pending impotence, I'm going to grab you the first chance I get, and both our clothes are immediately coming off. If you resist, try to escape, I'll get Linda to help me. I think by the way that she was able to come up with the three-way relationship plan on her own, you may bring out the kinky side of her a little, and I get the feeling she may enjoy helping me strip you, as long as you're just being reluctant and not seriously resisting. She'd turn on me in an instant and side with you if you were."

Then Jeff, looking at Matt and then Linda, and judging that delaying things would only give Matt time to become more frightened, said,

"If you're still willing and ready to try, just place your hands on Linda's shoulders, close your eyes, and go with the flow. Trust me; I've got you."

Linda moved close to Matt so their fronts were pressed together, kissed him on the cheek, and then whispered in his ear,

"Don't be frightened, Matt. It's just me, and I told you before I don't bite.

"I love you, and I know you love Jeff and me. I want to have your baby, and together with Jeff's help, the three of us will have a baby together.

"Jeff loves you so much and wants you to have a chance to be a father. He'll help you get through this. You're in his hands now – can't you feel him stimulating and guiding you?

"You know he's hyper-protective of you, will look for any signs that you're becoming too uncomfortable or overwhelmed, and won't let anything bad happen to you. Hopefully, you can relax a little and, trust him, feel safe in his hands.

Thomas Willard © 2023

Matt, suddenly feeling a lot less frightened and now fully aroused by Jeff's manipulations, said,

"Thanks, Linda. I think whatever Jeff's doing is working and starting to have a huge effect on me. He's got me relaxed and all-horned up. He knows how to push my buttons. I won't open my eyes, but my fear is gone. I'm just worried that I might hurt you; I have no idea what I'm doing."

Linda, relieved now and smiling, said,

"Jeff's an expert, and I'm kind of built for this, so no worries about hurting me. I told you before that you and Jeff are built the same everywhere, and Jeff is the perfect size for me.

"Don't worry if I get excited, start to pant, and say things like, "Oh, God!" or "Yes, yes!" It's just me letting you and Jeff know you're doing a good job. And near the end, I'll probably start kissing you in a different way than Jeff does. It's just me approaching orgasm. Woman's orgasms aren't like men's, which are over in an instant, leaving a pool of evidence behind.

Thomas Willard © 2023

"Our orgasms are more subtle, leaving our private parts wet and quivering, and can last for several minutes. And unlike men, we can orgasm multiple times without needing a pause to recover."

Jeff, having stimulated Matt to full arousal and inserted him into Linda, began squeezing Matt's butt with his left hand in a rhythm to get him to thrust. Linda quickly responded and started moaning and writhing, too.

Jeff's right hand was all over Matt's front and back, and he began kissing Matt on the neck and cheeks. As he felt Matt begin building towards an orgasm, Jeff switched to using both hands to squeeze Matt's butt. Then, to get Matt to thrust even harder, he used a finger of his right hand to press on Matt's perineum, or taint, something he'd never done before.

The result was nearly instantaneous. With the new sensation, Matt began to thrust much deeper and began to moan. Linda also responded and began kissing Matt on the mouth.

With a final deep thrust and a loud, guttural moan, Matt climaxed hard, pushing Linda over the edge and causing her to reach an orgasm of her own.

Breathing hard, with his eyes still closed, Matt found Linda's cheek and gently kissed her.

Jeff, who'd been like a man possessed, working at Matt's groin level, manipulating him to orgasm, straightened up and found Matt's face and tenderly kissed him before finding Linda's and passionately kissing her on the lips.

Matt remained on his knees with his eyes closed while Jeff removed his semi-erect penis from Linda, then dried it with a towel.

Then Matt opened his eyes and found Jeff staring back at him. Jeff kissed him on the lips, dried Matt's stomach with the towel, then said,

"There you go. Good as new."

Linda kissed Matt on the cheek, then said,

"That was unbelievable, Matt. I hope you're doing OK now."

Matt answered by hugging Linda and Jeff together, then kissing them both on the cheek, saying,

"Thanks, that was amazing. You both made it so easy for me. I wasn't frightened at all once we got started."

Then Matt turned to Jeff and said,

"You pushed all my buttons, some I didn't know I had before," then smiling, added, "I know how you like to keep things even. I can't wait to push your buttons the same way now. Come on big guy, it's your turn to make love to Linda," getting a fearful, whimpered, "Ahh!" from Jeff in return, and with Linda laughing, thinking, "This could be fun!"

Jeff made love to Linda, receiving a final extra boost from Matt's right-hand middle finger to put him over the top and letting out a loud groan, and then fell back exhausted, quickly falling asleep.

Thomas Willard © 2023

Matt gently straddled Jeff's injured leg high up, resting the weight of his leg and his erect penis on Jeff's thigh, and Linda straddled Jeff's other leg with her own. Matt gently stroked Jeff's hair while Linda tenderly rubbed his chest.

As Jeff predicted, the two soon began bonding while exchanging intimate details about Jeff and were now completely comfortable being naked together.

After a few minutes, Linda changed the subject to her sharing Jeff with Matt.

"Matt, I think you're worried that it's not fair for me to have to share Jeff with you.

"But you have it backward. You have a much bigger claim to Jeff than I do. First, you two were in a relationship before Jeff and I met. I knew that from the beginning and was more than fine with it; I wanted it to continue; I knew you needed each other.

"And you're going to bristle when I say this, but you've saved his life countless times, risking your own each time. I know

Jeff's saved yours, too, so you think things are even on that score. But they aren't.

"When Jeff told me about that last rescue - you pushing him to safety in Korea - even I knew how insanely risky that was. Jeff's body knows, too. That's why it shut down until Jeff found a way to be with you forever.

"You ask so little of him physically and emotionally; it won't be a problem for him to satisfy both you and me. And he has so much love in him that we can easily share him. Together I think we can make him the happiest guy in the world, which is something I know we both want for him. Whenever he makes love to me after he's been with you, he's Jeff-times-two, almost more than I can handle.

"But there is something else, something that most guys don't know about. Every month, I go through a cycle and have my period. It's nature's way of placing a new lining in a woman's womb to provide a place for a fertilized egg to nurture and grow into a baby.

Thomas Willard © 2023

"At the peak of my cycle, as I am now, I'm the most fertile, and conditions are best for me to become pregnant. Emotionally, I'm raring to go and full of desire. I can be flirty and try my best to be alluring to Jeff.

"But two weeks from now, in the depth of my cycle, the opposite will be true. I'll be awash in hormones, irritable and moody, my body will ache, and I'll have cramps. I'll feel undesirable, and the last thing I'll want is to have sex with Jeff or anyone else. I'll crave gentle affection, some peace and quiet, and a dimly lit room.

But the world goes on, and I have a job and a family to take care of, so I'll get up and do the best I can. Luckily, I work with a lot of women, all experiencing the same thing but not at the same time, and we help each other out.

"I'm also lucky to have such a considerate husband like Jeff. He knows my cycle and steps up his game when he thinks I need more help, taking on more care of Mikey, doing the cooking and house cleaning, and trying to let me get some extra quiet rest in the bedroom.

"He also tries to be comforting and affectionate, making me tea or bringing me a hot water bottle. But women are skittish during their time of the month – I think it's wired into us – and get nervous if a husband gets too affectionate, thinking it can lead to sex, something we don't want.

"That's where having you in our relationship would help. I know you'd help Jeff with Mikey and the chores. But you'd also be there to take care of Jeff's other needs – his need to be intimate with you, but also, just his need to have sex when I'm out of commission.

"So, you can see, for at least half the month, you could have Jeff all to yourself, though halfway through my cycle, I might want to watch you two together, as long as I didn't have to participate. And the other two weeks, the three of us would be trying to have a baby together.

Thomas Willard © 2023

"Sharing Jeff with you would not be a problem but a blessing to me and would make my life easier. And I would be very happy knowing that both Jeff and you were together."

Matt tried to absorb all this, then said,

"Linda, you know I don't agree that I have more of a claim to Jeff than you. But maybe we can compromise. I didn't know about your cycle. I know it must have been embarrassing for you to talk to me about it," then added, trying to keep things even, "like me or Jeff discussing masturbation with you.

"What if we go with the First Dibs rule? I'll try to learn your cycle from Jeff, but I don't think he or I will ever know it well enough to know on a given day how you're feeling about watching Jeff and me being affectionate with each other, or even having sex, or participating in having sex with both of us or just Jeff.

"You always have First Dibs on Jeff. You're out of commission half the time, so it's only fair that you have the first claim to him when you are feeling up to having sex. And if you are only in the mood for some erotic entertainment, Jeff and I will gladly put on a show for you anytime. But if you need to be left alone, just give us the high sign, and we'll quietly disappear into the next room until you're feeling better and call us back.

"You're the woman, the one experiencing a cycle, and should be in charge of all this. Jeff and I are the same all month long and should follow how you're feeling daily.

"We're kind of thick when it comes to stuff like this, though. Together, we need to develop a system, so Jeff and I know how to behave. Maybe a flippable color-coded series of panels, like paint samples, that you could casually display on your headboard would work, or a color-coded nightgown?"

Jeff, who'd been pretending to be asleep for the past few minutes, eavesdropping on the conversation while enjoying the physical attention still being paid to him by Matt and Linda, smiled on hearing Matt's engineering solution for displaying Linda's intimate arousal status for all the world to see.

Thomas Willard © 2023

He fully awoke, and thinking he'd try to rescue Linda before Matt suggested a neon sign as a solution, said,

"You two seem to be getting along pretty well. You haven't been sharing any of my personal secrets, I hope."

Linda and Matt smiled at each other, then Linda said,

"Only that you called Matt's name out in your sleep last night when you had a wet dream," causing Matt to laugh and Jeff to pull the sheet and blankets over his head, with a burning-faced Jeff thinking, "Oh, no! I'm in big trouble now."

#

CHAPTER 2 – FAMILY WINGMEN

A DAD'S INTUITION

Linda had selected that Saturday afternoon to try to become

pregnant based on her basal temperature and an estimate of the day

she'd ovulate. She knew the science suggested they'd have the best

chance of success if she and Matt had sex beginning five days

before ovulation and up to two days after.

Matt, however, completely unfamiliar with the mechanics

of pregnancy, thought it was a one-and-done deal and started asking Linda every day, and sometimes more than once a day, if she knew if she was pregnant yet.

So, Linda, thinking Matt was adorable, being so naive, took time to explain to him that it didn't work that way and that it might take several months of trying, using every golden opportunity, for her to become pregnant.

Matt always insisted that Jeff have sex with Linda after he'd finished donating and had come up with a crazy theory that if Linda did become pregnant, Jeff could still be the father. His idea was that Jeff's swimmers were more clever than his and would hitch a ride to the egg, arrive all rested, and win the race to fertilize the egg.

Linda and Jeff thought Matt's ideas were cute and didn't want to discourage him by throwing cold water on them. But when just a few days after their first attempt, Linda started experiencing morning sickness, followed by tenderness in her breasts, Linda started to reconsider. Then, when she missed her next period, her instincts and earlier pregnancy experience told her she needed to visit a doctor. When her tests came back a week later confirming she was pregnant, Linda and Jeff were shocked. But maybe they shouldn't have been: Linda had gotten pregnant quickly the first time, on their honeymoon.

Matt, though, not knowing any better, and remembering how quickly Linda had become pregnant after she and Jeff were married, thought that was how things were supposed to work and was more convinced than ever that Jeff was the father.

On 10 November 1952, Linda gave birth to a healthy, chestnut-haired, hazel-eyed baby girl. Since all the members of Linda and Jeff's families were blond-haired and blue-eyed, and girls were rare in Jeff's family, Matt reluctantly accepted that he was the father, saying that his swimmers must have cheated. Frank, though, was beside himself as he held the baby and thought how closely she resembled his wife, Kathryn, and Matt. When Linda and Jeff said they'd named the baby Kathryn Rose after Matt and Jeff's moms, Matt and his dad hugged each other, then hugged and kissed Linda and Jeff while they all wept with joy.

Thomas Willard © 2023

Linda asked Matt to sit in a rocking chair and hold the baby. Matt, who had never allowed himself to hope that he could actually become a father, instantly bonded with his new baby girl, and started rocking back and forth, trying to gently speak to and comfort his new daughter through his tears, which only grew worse when he had to hand the baby back to the nurse when visiting hours were over.

#

GAINFULLY EMPLOYED

Back in March 1952, Matt was about to complete his 20-month active-duty obligation and needed to decide what he wanted to do next, both militarily and work-wise.

If he did nothing, his military status would revert to being a member of the US Air Force Active Reserves. But that didn't appeal to him as much now that Jeff was no longer a member. And he could apply for his old job flying for MIT's Rad Lab, now MIT Lincoln Labs, or try to get an engineering job with Jeff at

Raytheon, though he wasn't sure how Jeff would feel about him 'clinging' to him like that.

So, Matt, always unsure of his feelings, asked Jeff to help him decide.

To Matt's surprise, Jeff had already begun thinking about Matt's – really Matt and Jeff's - future and about how Matt's decisions could affect their relationship. Jeff, conflicted, not wanting to decide for Matt, offered his thoughts.

"Matt, these are just my initial ideas. I expect you to push back and argue for what you want and not let me overly influence you.

"First, as far as flying for the Air Force Reserves anymore goes, I can't help it, but I'm not going to be very supportive of that; I'm too scared for you and just too plain selfish.

"The Reserve's aircraft are always going to be cutting-edge, pushing the safety boundaries. And as a member of the Active Reserves, you'd likely be called back to active duty to serve another tour in Korea. I'd be worried sick the whole time you were gone, plus, I don't think I could stand you being away from me for a week, let alone a whole year, and neither could Linda, Mikey, or your dad.

"I know you love flying, and you are the best pilot in the Air Force, so maybe I'm exaggerating the risks. But I'm selfish and don't want you to fly for the military or to be away from home for any extended period ever again. I don't feel the same way about you flying commercially, like for the airlines, MIT, or Raytheon, though.

"As far as work goes, I'd love to work with you at the same company and on the same projects. And I'd be clinging to you, not the other way around.

"But it might not be wise right now. The social environment has changed since WWII. Men that are in male-male relationships that were once tolerated, overlooked, and sometimes even encouraged during the war are now being persecuted and even prosecuted. Some busy-body at work might report us as being too close.

Thomas Willard © 2023

"And now, to have a job in the government or the defense industry - working for companies like Raytheon or Lincoln Labs – you need a security clearance, and it's against the law for a person to hold a clearance that is a homosexual; the government claims they'd be subject to blackmail, ignoring the fact that they'd only be subject to blackmail because the government created the ban on homosexuals working in the government or defense in the first place. To get a clearance, the FBI thoroughly investigates your background and even administers a lie detector test.

"Thanks to Spiegel, there is no record of too-close of a bond between us. And those in command that might have suspected that we bonded, I think, would protect us, as long as they didn't have to lie. Doolittle even gave me an unsolicited job reference; you can't get a better character reference than that.

"Still, it might be better if we separate our paper trail a little at work, working on similar projects but for different companies located around Hanscom AFB. Your living with us here in Concord could be disguised by your using your dad's address as your legal address. And our closeness could be explained by our time in the service together and our business partnership: you don't know it yet, but you're a half-partner in a real estate development company, selling one-acre housing lots here in Concord."

After Jeff finished, Matt took a moment to digest all that Jeff said before responding.

"When you gave me my ring, you promised to make all the tough moral calls in our relationship, and you have come through again, saving me from my worst instincts.

"You've put a lot of thought into this plan, and I agree with everything you said. I'm going to follow all your recommendations, starting with resigning from the Active Reserves. That will still put me in the inactive Reserves, but I'll resign my commission if they come after me for another tour in Korea.

"I'm going to apply to Lincoln Labs for a position that requires a pilot with an engineering degree to get both engineering and practical experience designing and testing airborne radar and missile systems. I'm sure we'll still end up working together on some projects.

"And as far as being a business partner with you, I can't imagine what use I'd be to you, but I'm all in. You'll need to teach me a few buzz words to throw around, though, in case I'm ever questioned about it."

Jeff, feeling guilty that he might have talked Matt into his plan, said,

"Are you sure you want this plan, Matt? It's pretty far from your original idea."

Smiling in relief, Matt said,

"I'm positive. The plan is perfect, and you've thought of everything. I only feel guilty for dumping yet another moral dilemma on you. Thanks for rescuing me again."

Jeff, knowing they could always modify the plan, relaxed about overly influencing Matt's decision but then raised a final concern.

"Matt, I just have one more worry. You're very honest, and except for hiding your feelings, you have trouble lying.

"From now on, I want you to adopt my view of what's honorable when it comes to lying about your personal information.

"No one – no government, company, or religious investigator - has the right to ask you about your personal, private life or thoughts. If they do, you have the right to lie your ass off, and I want you to do just that with no tell-tale blushing.

"Think of it this way. How would they answer you if you asked them a private question, like when was the last time they masturbated, and what fantasy were they thinking about while they were doing it? Every one of them would either say it was none of your business or would lie through their teeth and say that they had never masturbated before in their life.

"If you think as I do – that those types of questions violate your right to privacy, and you have no moral obligation to answer them truthfully – you should have no trouble passing an interview or lie detector test. We'll practice ahead of time by asking each

Thomas Willard © 2023

other the most intimate questions we can imagine to desensitize ourselves."

Matt applied for and was awarded a combined pilot/engineering position at Lincoln Labs starting in May, becoming a Member of the Technical Staff, and began by collaborating with Draper Labs on the development of an inertial guidance system for aircraft.

In September, Jeff started his systems engineering job at Raytheon. After practice sessions beforehand, Matt and Jeff both passed an FBI investigation, interview, and lie detector test and had each received an active secret clearance by January 1953.

#

DANCE CODE

By mid-September 1952, two months after his final surgery, the bones in Jeff's leg had healed.

Though he had no pain or loss of mobility, possibly out of fear of reinjury, he still favored his strong leg and had a slight limp. Matt had tried to build the strength up in Jeff's leg as he recovered, exercising with him in the pool and walking with him several miles each day.

But there remained an obvious difference in size between the muscles of Jeff's left, or strong leg, and his right. The result was that Jeff had trouble walking fast or running, but maybe more importantly to Jeff, dancing. Linda would be pregnant for another two months, but Jeff had set a goal for himself that he hadn't shared with Matt; to be able to dance with Linda once she'd recovered from having the baby, hopefully by Thanksgiving.

By the end of October, with little sign of improvement, Jeff was becoming discouraged. He wanted desperately to be able to surprise Linda and dance with her once she was able. But Jeff's dancing standard was so high, and his progress so slow, that he knew now, he'd never make it in time.

Jeff managed to put all of that aside when Linda delivered a healthy baby girl in early November, celebrating with Matt and Frank, laughing and crying with joy when they were first allowed

Thomas Willard © 2023

to visit Linda and the baby in the maternity ward. He was especially happy for Matt, who was overwhelmed and unable to speak near the end of their visit.

Later that night, when Matt and Jeff had returned to Concord from the hospital, and with Mikey at his grandparents' home in Lowell, they settled on the couch in the living room, with an arm draped over each other's shoulder.

Matt, still emotional, needed to say something to Jeff, so he dug deep and pushed himself, resolving not to cry until he finished.

"Jeff. You are an extraordinary person. I hope you know that.

"I don't think there is another living soul that would have done what you did for me, given me this chance to experience being a father. That wasn't you just being generous. That was you unselfishly letting me be a stand-in for you, of your wanting me to experience the joy you had having Mikey, and it has to be the greatest gift anyone has ever given.

Thomas Willard © 2023

"I didn't think it was possible to love you more, but I love you so much right now it hurts that I don't know how to say or show it."

Jeff, sensing Matt was hanging on by a thread, pulled him into an embrace and said,

"Matt, I'm so glad you got to experience being a dad; you have no idea how happy that made me. You told me when we were in Marblehead that I'd make a great dad, but I've always thought you'd make a great one, too." Then Jeff tenderly kissed Matt on the lips.

They held each other in their arms for about a half hour until Matt recovered his composure a little. It was only then that Matt sensed a sadness in Jeff and called him on it.

"Jeff, are you hiding something from me? Are you injured or sick, or did I do or say anything to upset you?

"Don't tell me that it's nothing; I know better. I'm much better at hiding things than you are and know all the signs. You have ten seconds to tell me what's wrong, or I'm going to go berserk, either tickling you to death until you give me an answer or wailing my guts out; I never know which way I'm going to go."

Then, after considering what might be bothering Jeff, Matt asked,

"Are you feeling sad from not being the father? It's my fault for giving you false hope; I'm so sorry," before completely breaking down and sobbing.

Jeff immediately started comforting Matt.

"No, it has nothing to do with you. I didn't lie; I'm thrilled that you're a dad. And I never thought your "my-swimmer's-hitching-a-ride" theory was plausible; Linda and I just thought it was cute, so no worries, you didn't give me any false hope.

Then, in a quiet, tender voice, Jeff said, "Your willingness to have a baby with Linda saved my marriage, not from any pressure coming from Linda, but from the pressure I was putting on myself. Now, after having another baby, and especially because it's a girl, Linda is over the moon, and her "baby fever" urges are more than satisfied. I don't feel nearly as inadequate for being

Thomas Willard © 2023

sterile or that I'm robbing Linda of her chance for fulfillment, both as a wife and a mother.

"Linda's still young – two years younger than me - and can safely have another baby for at least another ten years. I haven't given up hope, and if she wants to try again, I'll do everything I can to make that happen short of surgery, which could leave me worse off than I am.

"There are things you can do to increase your sperm count, like reducing your stress level, eliminating alcohol, eating right, wearing loose-fitting boxers, taking lukewarm showers instead of hot baths, and taking vitamins along with a zinc supplement; I'm doing them all. Plus, my damaged testicles could repair on their own.

"But you've taken the pressure off me and made Linda and a lot of other people very happy in the process. I can't thank you enough."

Matt said, "Promise if you do get Linda pregnant, and it's a boy, you'll name him after yourself, Jeff, Jr."

Thomas Willard © 2023

Jeff didn't like the idea of naming a son after himself, thinking it would be the height of conceit, but incapable of denying Matt anything, he said,

"I always let Linda choose the baby's name. After all, she's done all the work. And you have to admit she's pretty good at it; she came up with Kathryn Rose on her own.

"I'll tell you what. You can let Linda know that your vote is for the baby to be named after me, and I won't lobby against it. Is that a deal?" getting a satisfied nod in agreement from Matt.

Jeff, still not wanting to tell Matt what was bothering him, but knowing from Matt's expression that he wasn't going to let up trying to find the reason, or would blame himself if he couldn't find one, finally relented and told Matt what was wrong.

"Matt, you always blame yourself for everything. But you haven't done anything wrong; it's me. I've done this to myself by making unrealistic plans for Linda and me."

Then Jeff described his plan to surprise Linda after she had recovered, maybe on Thanksgiving, by dancing with her the way he used to, even if it was only to slow songs.

He explained that he had always used dancing as foreplay in his lovemaking with Linda – there's a name for it, choreophilia - and that it had never failed to get Linda aroused.

Then he quoted George Bernard Shaw, saying, "Dance is the vertical expression of a horizontal desire legalized by music."

Jeff had learned to perform sexually without dancing first while he was injured, accepting that the passion between him and Linda would be lessened but expected it to be a temporary change. Now, he was concerned he may never dance again, and with desperation and fear in his voice said,

"I'm worried that if I'm not able to dance with Linda soon, she will find another dancing partner and my marriage will be over."

Matt listened to Jeff with a mix of compassion and concern. He knew that Jeff's anguish was irrational, that Linda had no intention of leaving him, and certainly not for something as trivial as a better dancing partner. But he didn't want to be dismissive of Jeff's worries: they may not be based on reality, but they were real enough to Jeff.

"OK, Jeff. Thanks for telling me what's bothering you.

"I don't think you have anything to worry about. Linda doesn't want to leave you for any reason, especially not to be with a better dancer. She's crazy in love with you, now more than ever.

"I think you've convinced yourself that she only loved you for your dancing, and now that you can't dance as well, she is going to leave you. Linda's not violent, but I bet she'd punch you in the arm if you told her that.

"I loved watching you dance and all the times we got to dance together. Do you think I'm going to leave you because you're not the same dancer you once were? At thirty years old, who is?

"I only feel bad that you're not able to do something that you used to love to do, the same as flying. Do you think I'm going to leave you because you're no longer able to fly, too? If you say yes, I'll punch you in the arm myself; I just got done telling you I love you so much it hurts.

"Don't you think you might be blowing Linda's love for dancing out of proportion? She's not the one with a dancing fetish, but you might be. I agree she loves dancing, but it's not just dancing; it's dancing with you; there's a big difference.

"If you decide to dance with her on Thanksgiving, you won't have to do any fancy steps or even move at all to make her happy. Just hold her in your arms, as you did with me in Romsey. If there's a heaven, that's what it will feel like."

Matt's attempt at comforting Jeff and allaying his fears somehow backfired, and Jeff was now more upset than ever and was openly sobbing.

So, Matt switched tactics. He held Jeff and let him cry it out for a few minutes before saying, in an as soothing and reassuring voice as he could manage,

Thomas Willard © 2023

"It'll be all right, OK? Maybe I'm wrong, and you're right to feel the way that you do.

"So, what's the plan? I'm game for anything. Between the two of us, I think we can come up with a solution."

Jeff, now a little calmer but still upset and discouraged, with resignation said,

"There is no solution; it's hopeless. I was already feeling like I wasn't satisfying Linda enough before she became pregnant. I can't think of what I can do to make up for the loss of dancing."

Matt thought for a moment and then offered a plan.

"Your leg isn't quite up to snuff, but I'm sure it's going to be soon. In the meantime, you can borrow my legs; I'll be your stand-in.

"Linda keeps telling us that we have the same body. And I've had sex with her, so dancing with her, no matter how erotic it gets, should be much less intimate than what we've already done.

"You've taught me at least ten of your dance steps. I think if we practice some more, you could train me well enough that

Linda won't be able to tell the difference between us, at least in the dark, but with one exception.

" I can learn your steps, but there is no way I'll ever learn how to string the steps together and choreograph a dance like you can. But we could come up with a code, and you could give me hand signals telling me what step to use next and when to switch. How's that?"

Jeff, flabbergasted, could only say, "You'd do that for me?"

Matt, smiling and displaying his ring, said,

"You own me, all of me, including my legs. Of course, I'd do that for you.

"You have to promise, though, not to disappear on me after we get Linda all wound up, or I could be in serious trouble."

A much-relieved Jeff said,

"Thank you, Matt, for coming up with your plan. I know it's crazy, like all our plans, but Linda is good at looking the other way, ignoring any flaws in our plans, and will give us a pass just for trying, so I think your plan will work."

Thomas Willard © 2023

Matt, feeling a little guilty, sheepishly said, "Don't thank me too much; I'm making out like a bandit here. I get to dance with you every day for the next two weeks," getting a big hug from Jeff, signaling that that was just fine with him.

They celebrated Thanksgiving at Frank's house in Swampscott, with Matt and Jeff helping prepare the dinner and cleaning up afterward while minding the children, leaving Linda to rest in the living room's rocker in front of the fireplace with the two sleeping dogs by her feet.

When they got back to Concord around 9:00 pm, Matt and Jeff put Mikey and Kathryn to bed. Linda was doing some dishes when Jeff came into the kitchen and told her that he and Matt had a surprise for her waiting in the living room.

When Linda entered the room, she found Matt in the center, holding out his hand, as Jeff pushed play on the record player.

Matt whispered into Linda's ear, "Try to pretend it's Jeff dancing with you. He really wanted it to be with him, you have no idea how much, but he couldn't risk you seeing him stumble," as

Matt did his best impression of Jeff, watching for his hand signals, pressed close to Linda, and dancing to Dinah Washington's latest hit, the slow song "Teach Me Tonight," and with Linda's eyes locked on Jeff's

When the song finished, Matt brought Linda over to Jeff, who then passionately kissed her. Smiling, Matt fake-yawned and said he was going to bed in the guest room, leaving the already half-naked married couple all to themselves.

As he was drifting off to sleep, Matt thought, "Ok, maybe it was a crazy plan. But sometimes "crazy" does work. I wouldn't be a dad otherwise."

#

ROAD TO RICHES

When Jeff first considered buying the 60-acre Jones Farm in Concord, MA, in June 1947, it wasn't just for its farm potential.

He had family in Illinois that were successful small farmers, growing wheat, corn, hay, and fruits and vegetables, and had been taught which soil conditions were best suited for farming particular crops.

He could see that, unlike Illinois farmland, New England farmland was rocky and uneven, but knew that the farm's Paxton-type coarse-loamy topsoil was well suited for pastureland and growing hay and was particularly good for growing apples, which explained the extensive pear and apple orchards covering most of the farm, now substantially overgrown by brush from decades of neglect.

But Jeff's real interest in the farm was its potential for housing development.

Jeff could see that the area surrounding Hanscom AB was fast becoming the technological center of the US, with new companies like Raytheon, MITRE, and Lincoln Labs – all affiliated with Harvard University or MIT – leading the way.

The completion of the semicircular Route 128 highway, running from Gloucester in the north to Canton in the south, encircling metro Boston, also designated The Yankee Division

Highway and referred to in a 1955 *Business Week* article as "The Magic Semicircle," helped drive the "Massachusetts Miracle." Already by 1958, the just-finished highway had to be widened from four lanes to six.

In 1957, there were 99 new high-tech companies located along Route 128, employing 17,000 employees; by 1965, there were 574 companies; and in 1973, there were 1,212.

Jeff, while working at MIT's Radiation Lab at Hanscom, had foreseen this rapid development and realized that all these new company employees - most with high-paying jobs - were going to need housing, and knew that, at a time when there was already a housing shortage, the demand for new housing was going to be enormous, especially in towns close to Hanscom, like Concord.

So, Jeff bought the Jones farm, intending to keep the ten acres the colonial-era house and later-era barn and the best orchards were situated on and to divide the remaining 50 acres into one-acre housing lots.

Jeff hadn't initially invited Matt to join his business venture, not wanting to risk Matt's money on his speculative idea. But when Matt gave him all his savings so he could avoid foreclosure, Jeff considered him an equal partner. By then, in early 1952, Jeff could already see that his prediction of massive economic development in the area surrounding Hanscom was becoming a reality.

Matt had saved Jeff's initial investment by giving Jeff all of his savings. Now Jeff intended to repay Matt, not by repaying the loan – which Matt considered a gift – but by making both him and Matt wealthy.

In May of 1952, before the development rush, Jeff applied for and got the farm re-zoned for housing development. Then he waited, watching the price of one-acre housing lots in the Concord area rise, starting from $2500 per acre and initially doubling each year. When, in 1958, the price reached over $60,000 per acre, Jeff sold all the lots to a real estate developer, with Jeff and Matt's company, Wingmen Associates, Limited, netting a profit of $3,000,000.

Jeff waited until all the documents were processed and the money deposited into the company's checking account before asking Matt to meet him for dinner that same Friday after work at Matt's favorite restaurant in Concord, the Colonial Inn, built in 1716.

After they'd been seated and had ordered dinner and were sipping a beer – alcohol now being a rarity for Jeff – Jeff, with a grin, asked,

"Matt, do you remember when you bailed me out and gave me all your savings, rescuing me from foreclosure and bankruptcy?"

Matt, uncomfortable, not even willing to acknowledge that Jeff had ever been in financial trouble, just groaned and said,

"Why do you want to talk about that? Everything is perfect now. That was just a bump in the road; you're well past that. You probably own the farm outright by now."

Thomas Willard © 2023

That caused Jeff to break into a big smile.

"I told you then, Matt, you owned half the farm. And yes, we do; we now own the farm outright. See, we received the title today," as Jeff handed the title to Matt to read.

Matt, thinking that was the reason for their celebrating, raised his glass in a toast, saying, "To freedom," before clanging his glass with Jeff's.

Jeff, though, wasn't finished.

"Matt, I don't want to deceive you. The farm is much smaller now, only ten acres. See, read the property description on the title."

Matt, not concerned about the size of the farm, said, "We don't care. I'm sure you kept the best parts. The bank can have the rest."

Then Jeff, not wanting to tease Matt any further, said,

"The bank doesn't own the rest of the farm. I sold the 50 acres, in one-acre lots, through our company, Wingmen Associates. Remember the paper I had you sign, forming our partnership? You own half the profits from the sales, and half the remainder of the farm, what's in the property description on the title."

Jeff pulled Matt's joint-business account checkbook from his pocket and handed it to Matt, saying,

"Here, this is yours; our balance is $3,000,000. We are both millionaires thanks to your unquestioning generosity."

Matt, in full alarm mode, said,

"No, that's not right! You did all the work; I only gave you a little money. You can pay me back; how's that?"

Jeff, smiling, holding out his MIT ring, gently said,

"You said what's mine is yours, and yours is mine.

"We share everything, including the clothes we're wearing, so you better get used to it; we're both millionaires. And I'm buying dinner. No arguments or I'll sic Linda on you," getting a groan of resignation from Matt in response.

When they got home an hour later, Jeff called Frank to give him the good news and to let Frank congratulate Matt, which

Thomas Willard © 2023

sealed the deal and left Matt no chance to find a loophole in the arrangement – he knew his dad would side with Jeff.

After they'd hung up, Jeff pulled Matt into a hug and tenderly said, "Do you think I would want to be rich without you for a second?

"You've been the silent partner in our business, but without your money, there would be no business. You made it happen just as much as me and deserve half the profits.

"Look, Matt, you took the same risks as me and could have lost everything. So, we're even, right, just the way we like it?" kissing Matt on the cheek and then hugging him closely before leading Matt to Matt's bedroom: Jeff knew Matt was overwhelmed and would need to be held for the rest of the night to give him a chance to cry it all out and get over the shock.

When Matt awoke early the next morning, he found Jeff awake, staring back at him, still holding him tight.

Matt said, in a firm, somber voice,

"I'll only accept this financial arrangement if you agree to some conditions.

"First, I assume we've retained a company lawyer, so I want him to draw up a will for me as soon as possible, giving you everything I own if something happens to me, or if something happens to you first, to give everything to Linda and the kids.

"Second, you agree to quietly help anyone in Linda's or your family that runs into a rough patch financially. You never need to ask me; just help them in any way that you can.

"And third, you remain in charge of all the finances. Your business judgment got us here, and I more than trust you with my life, let alone money, so you never need to ask for my input or permission to do anything."

Jeff thought about Matt's conditions and agreed to them all but wanted to modify the last one.

"Matt, I agree to all your conditions, but I'm bothered by the last one and hope you'll let me make a small change.

"I'll stay in charge and come up with the overall financial strategy, but I'll want your input and will keep you aware of everything that I'm doing. But like you teaching me how to sail, I want you to know how to handle the business stuff a little, in case something does happen to me, plus I don't like having a skill that you don't have.

"I'll make a deal with you. I'll teach you some business stuff, and you teach me how to play the piano, at least the basics. I've always wanted to learn to play, and I admire you a lot for being able to do it. I remember you playing "The White Cliffs of Dover" at The Tudor Rose in Romsey. It gave me goosebumps then and still does."

Matt agreed to both the change and the deal, then enthusiastically told Jeff,

"You know the piano is considered part of the rhythm section of a band. You have so much rhythm in you that you'd make a great piano player."

Thomas Willard © 2023

Jeff, sensing Matt was now on board with their financial arrangement, began telling Matt about some of the ideas he had for using a small part of their money.

He wanted to continue renovating the farmhouse, upgrading the electrical and heating systems, modernizing and expanding the kitchen, adding two more bathrooms and modernizing the existing one, and adding two more bedrooms, bringing the total to six. The changes would allow more space for their families to visit and provide Frank with his own room in the farmhouse.

Jeff also wanted to remodel the barn, keeping a small section for farm storage but creating two in-law apartments that would allow for larger groups of their families to visit, and Frank a bigger space away from the farmhouse if he found he needed more privacy.

Like Matt, Jeff wanted Frank to retire early. He thought one way to get him to do that was to keep Frank busy. He knew Frank liked gardening and thought they could ask him to run their microfarm for them, looking after the small orchards, the vegetable garden, and even starting a small vineyard growing Concord grapes.

Jeff's family loved Massachusetts, especially the beach in Swampscott. Jeff thought he could lure his family to visit more by offering a place to stay in Swampscott, though he knew his mom would gladly make the trip just for the chance to hug Kathryn Rose; Rose loved her namesake so much.

The problem was the house in Swampscott only had two bedrooms and one bath. Jeff was hoping he and Matt could talk Frank into letting them pay for an extension to the house, adding two more bedrooms and at least one more bath. The additional bedrooms would also allow Jeff, Linda, Matt, Mikey, and Kathryn to stay at Frank's for multiple nights. Jeff was hoping the prospect of too much company and overbooking in Swampscott would help Frank to agree. If Jeff had his way, Frank would never eat another meal alone again unless by choice.

Jeff's final idea, which was an extension of his enticing-their-families-to-visit idea, was to get another, bigger boat. He loved Frank's boat as much as Frank and Matt did, but it was too small to carry all their immediate family members, let alone any visiting family. Jeff wanted to buy a larger sailboat, one capable of accommodating ten people in comfort for at least a week, and had the perfect name for her: the Kathryn Rose. He thought they should still keep the original boat, though, for sentimental reasons and more intimate sails, but that he and Matt should cover the maintenance and storage costs.

When Jeff finished and asked what he thought of his plans, a flabbergasted Matt broke down and, crying, started repeating over and over again, "Yes, yes, yes, to everything," while continuing to rain down kisses on Jeff's lips. Jeff decided that meant Matt was on board with his plans and started kissing Matt back, first with a rising passion, but then with a rising something else.

#

Thomas Willard © 2023

CHAPTER 3 — 15TH YEAR REUNION OF THE 55TH FIGHTER GROUP: DAY ONE

FIRST DANCE

The WWII-era hangar at San Luis Obispo County Regional Airport, formerly the Army's McChesney Field, had been temporarily converted into a dance hall. The live band, Les Elgart's Orchestra, was just finishing their first set with their hit song, "Bandstand Boogie." At 8:00 pm sharp, the Master of Ceremonies, the Group's former commanding officer, Colonel George T. Crowell, USAF, Retired, took to the makeshift stage.

He welcomed all the former Group members and their families of the 55th Fighter Group, 66th Fighter Wing, VIII Fighter Command, 8th Air Force, US Army Air Force - a P-38 fighter group stationed at Nuthampstead and Wormingford Airfields near Cambridge, England, during WWII - to their 15th-year reunion.

After taking some good-natured jibes at a few of his former subordinates, he announced that the live band would be back soon, but first, he wanted to play a recording by special request.

He looked out into the crowd and spotted two of his best former pilots, Matt Yetman and his close friend, Jeff Sullivan. Then, looking directly at Jeff's wife, Linda, standing next to Jeff, said, "He's all yours."

This announcement caused the crowd surrounding the dance floor to go wild with cheering and applause as Linda grabbed Matt's hand instead of Jeff's and led him to the center of the dance floor. Matt sensed a conspiracy unfolding but was powerless to stop it.

Matt's face was flushed as he held Linda in his arms, waiting for the music to begin. Colonel Crowell knew better than to wait any longer or risk Matt bolting. So, he quickly requested the crowd to be silent and then nodded for the music to start.

Dinah Washington's rendition of "Manhattan" began with a downbeat of strings. Matt took Linda's hand to lead, beginning awkwardly at first with small steps in a tight box, then slowly expanding the box as he began to relax and feel the music.

Linda sensed the change and moved her head to rest on Matt's shoulders, pulling him closer. The crowd, which had remained silent, now lost all control as they saw the pair embrace and cheered wildly again. The cheering caused Matt to stop moving and to look up in a panic at Jeff. But the crowd instinctively knew what to do. With or without a partner, everyone rushed to the dance floor, blocking any of Matt's escape routes. Matt and Linda were surrounded, lost in a sea of dancers, but since no one was watching the pair now, Matt calmed down and resumed dancing.

Thomas Willard © 2023

When the song finished, Matt, still flushed, returned Linda to Jeff, saying, "Thanks for the dance, Linda, that was great." Then, Matt turned to thank Jeff and shake his hand. But Jeff, who was grinning from ear-to-ear, and choking back tears, would have none of it. He grabbed Matt, first in a tight hug, then pulled Matt's head to his until they bumped, and then kissed the top of his head.

Jeff's 15-year-old son, Mike, had been watching this unfold with a group of teen friends at the back of the hangar; his 10-year-old sister, Kathryn, was back home keeping her grandfather, Frank, and the family's two dogs company.

One of the guys said, "Hey, it looks like your Uncle Matt has the hots for your mom," causing Mike to bristle.

When Mike saw Matt and his dad heading off to grab a beer, he approached his mother.

"Mom, what's up with that? Uncle Matt was all over you."

Linda smiled a little and said, "You know I always ask Matt to dance with me every chance that I get. He's a great dancer now, but he wasn't always. Your dad taught him everything he knows.

"Matt dances just like your dad used to before he injured his leg in Korea. Now, dancing with Matt is as close as I can get to dancing with your dad. If you notice, though, I only dance with Matt when your dad is there watching, and I never break eye contact with your dad.

"Trust me; there's no reason for you to worry. Your dad will explain it all soon when he thinks you're old enough to understand. Once you know the full story, who knows, you might ask Matt to teach you how to dance. Nothing would make your dad or me happier."

She tussled Mike's hair - which she knew he hated, especially in front of his friends - but did it anyway: a mother's prerogative. Then she compounded his embarrassment by hugging him, partly to hide the tears running down her face. All she could think of, for the millionth time, was, "Thank you, Matt."

#

Thomas Willard © 2023

CON JOB

Before Matt and Jeff reached the bar, two beers, discreetly purchased and placed on the bar, were waiting for them. Matt quietly accepted the anonymous gift, realizing that "the arrangement" was still in effect even after all these years. He inconspicuously raised his glass to quietly acknowledge whoever had bought the beers, sadly knowing he would never be able to return the favor. Jeff, though, was happy for the freebie, knowing it meant that all of the terms of "the arrangement" were still being honored.

Matt knew these displays of affection were genuine and not tied to any feelings of gratitude. But they were becoming increasingly harder to bare given his naturally reserved and introverted nature and were the main reason he had decided that this would be his last reunion.

Jeff had guessed that this would be Matt's last reunion and had confided this to Linda, who quietly reserved the opening dance

Thomas Willard © 2023

for her and Matt. That request had leaked out, though, and telegraphed to everyone that this would probably be the last time they would ever see Matt.

When Jeff learned that the word had spread, he asked everyone to re-swear their oath to never violate "the arrangement" Jeff had negotiated some 19 years earlier. All swore to abide by its terms fully.

Matt and Jeff had just started back to rejoin Linda when one of the Squadron's former pilots, Jon Martin, approached them. Billy Dempsey, also a former pilot, had just purchased a war surplus P-38 and had flown it to the airfield. He planned to give a little airshow the next day around noon.

This news was gut-wrenching to Matt. As far as he knew, he was the only one of the Squadron's members to have remained a professional pilot, working the past eleven years for Lincoln Labs.

He knew that even when new, with everything working perfectly, the P-38 was a demanding plane to fly, requiring many hours of practice for a pilot to remain competent. A surplus plane, with a suspect maintenance record, could, if anything went wrong, present a tough challenge for even the best of pilots, and Lieutenant Billy Dempsey had been the worst P-38 pilot in the Squadron, though he later became an Ace flying the P-51.

Matt excused himself, saying he needed to get some air, and left Jeff and Jon to fantasize about buying a surplus Warbird of their own.

He walked to the flight line and found Billy proudly displaying his vintage P-38, which Matt thought looked a little worse for wear, to a few Squadron members and their families. Billy beamed when he saw Matt approach and, after extolling Matt's flying virtues, in strict violation of "the arrangement," offered Matt the chance to climb into the cockpit. But to Billy's dismay, Matt was more interested in learning the condition and maintenance history of the plane and how many hours Billy had flying it.

Jeff suddenly became aware that Matt had slipped away. He now suspected that the slight grimace he'd noticed on Matt's face when Jon had given them the news about Billy's P-38 could only mean one thing. Jeff quickly made for the flight line, as fast as his weaker leg would allow, but his worst fears were soon realized when, from still a fair distance away, he saw Matt enthusiastically shaking Billy's hand, then slapping him on the back, something that he knew Matt normally would never do.

When he got closer to the group, he heard the news that he'd feared, that Matt had talked Billy into letting him fly the demonstration in the morning. Jeff knew that only Matt could have talked Billy out of flying the next day, and he knew that Matt, who had saved Billy's life countless times during the war, and who Billy idolized, was well aware of that, too.

Jeff also knew how good of an actor Matt could be and how determined he could be in trying to save someone from self-destruction. If Matt had played the "you owe me" card, no matter how subtly, it would have been the only time that Jeff knew of, and

Billy, more than anyone else in the Squadron, would be the most susceptible to it.

When Matt saw Jeff walking towards him, he told Billy he'd see him at 10:00 am: the flight was scheduled for noon, but he wanted plenty of time to do the pre-flight inspection of the plane. Then he quickly walked to meet Jeff to minimize the distance Jeff would have to walk back.

As Matt reached Jeff, he handed him his nearly full beer, saying,

"Here, you can finish this for me. I'll let you buy me one tomorrow when I get back."

Jeff, trying to hide his concern, said, "That's a deal."

They started to walk back to the hangar, but Matt thought Jeff was limping a little, so he wrapped his arm around him for support. Jeff wasn't having any trouble walking, though, but he gladly accepted the help: he needed to be physically close to Matt just then. Neither spoke for the rest of the way back.

Thomas Willard © 2023

Once they reached Linda and Mike, they listened to the band for a few minutes. After the band finished playing their hit, "Zing Went the Strings of My Heart," with Linda dancing mostly by herself, switching holding hands between a stationary Matt and Jeff, they decided it was time to leave: the next day was going to be a busy one.

Matt gave Linda and Jeff each a hug goodnight, but when he turned to pat Mike on the shoulder, Mike flinched and pulled away.

That crushed Matt, but he quickly buried his feelings like he always did. Only two people would have been able to detect the outward signs of Matt's reaction to Mike's rejection: Jeff and Linda. But they knew him well enough to know that he didn't want Mike rebuked. Whatever he'd done to make Mike angry, Matt wanted to work it out with Mike privately.

Matt loved Jeff and Linda so much that he didn't think it possible to love anyone more until he considered, just then, how much he loved Mike.

Thomas Willard © 2023

Matt had been busy with work lately, testing a lightweight, compact inertia guidance system for commercial jet airliner use, so he hadn't been able to spend as much time with Mike as he usually did. He thought that might be why Mike was so angry with him.

After tomorrow's flight, he'd ask Mike if they could go for a sail together when they got home, maybe to Gloucester, and he'd talk with Mike then to see if he could patch things up. But Matt knew he couldn't let this worry keep him up that night. Somehow, he thought he might need to be at his best the next day, and he hadn't felt that way for a very long time.

#

CHAPTER 4 - 15TH YEAR REUNION: DAY TWO: MID-MORNING

PRE-FLIGHT INSPECTION

At around 9:30 am the following day, Matt and Jeff met for breakfast at the coffee shop in the airfield's terminal building. Jeff had spent the night fuming over what he thought of as Billy's irresponsible stunt of bringing his decrepit P-38 to the reunion, forcing Matt to either watch a disaster unfold or step in and pull Billy's ass out of the fire again.

Jeff tried to talk Matt out of flying the demonstration, saying,

"He's an idiot! Has anyone checked to see if he even has a pilot's license?"

But Jeff knew that Matt was trapped: if he pushed Billy too hard, Billy would fly the demonstration himself.

Jeff got an agreement from Matt that if they found anything wrong with the plane during the pre-flight inspection, Matt would refuse to fly, and he'd try as hard as he could to get an A&P mechanic to declare the aircraft unairworthy, grounding it.

Jeff was more than satisfied and couldn't wait now to pre-flight the plane. He was on a mission. The P-38 was complex, and you could always find something wrong if you looked hard enough, and Jeff was going to look as hard as possible.

They left the coffee shop and arrived at the hangar just at 10:00 am to find Billy and one of the line mechanics opening the engine cowls for closer inspection. They had already removed all the inspection panels on the wings, twin booms, engine nacelles, and central gondola fuselage.

Jeff, still a little heated, said hello to Billy and nodded to the mechanic. Matt shook both Billy's and the mechanic's hands and then, looking at the mechanic, asked,

"So, how's she looking? Find anything major?"

Billy answered instead, saying they had just started the inspection a few minutes earlier and hadn't found any problems so far.

Jeff became a house-a-fire, roaming all over the plane, anywhere he could reach from the ground without having to kneel, looking for any apparent problems, hoping to find an obvious reason to ground the plane quickly.

But the more they looked, with four pairs of experienced eyes, the less likely it became that they were going to find any serious problems. Without partially disassembling the plane, as is done for a 100-hour inspection, or putting the plane up on jacks, necessary to inspect and test the undercarriage thoroughly, there was only so much that could be checked.

Thomas Willard © 2023

Jeff would have settled for a broken safety wire to ground the plane, but he couldn't even find that. His last hope was for a problem to surface during the engine run-up tests. If an oil pressure gauge fluttered the slightest, or a mag-check was low by only 10 rpm, he'd try to intimidate the mechanic into not signing the plane off.

They rolled the plane out of the hangar and began the run-up test. The engines, beginning with #1, the port engine, and then #2, the starboard engine, quickly started without any issues and sounded great.

After the engines were warmed up, both passed their mag and propeller checks. All the instruments were working properly, including the pressure gages, and the radio and navigation electronics were all working. Though the plane could use a paint job, it seemed in good shape mechanically.

What should have been good news, though, set Jeff off.

He lit into Billy, trying desperately to get him to cancel the demonstration. He at first tried to be moderately reasonable, arguing that most people who would have liked to see the show would be gone for the day, off sightseeing. They could see him take off when he flew home the next day.

When that didn't change Billy's mind, Jeff resorted to personal attacks, calling him the worst pilot, with the worst judgment he had ever met.

Billy and Jeff had tangled before back at Nuthampstead, when Billy, having been saved by Matt from an ME109 on his tail and frustrated that Matt, then only a sergeant pilot, hadn't accepted his invitation to join him in the Officer's Club for a beer to thank him, tried to pin the nickname "The Hermit" on Matt for his quiet ways. Jeff had overheard Billy's comments and became enraged. He jumped Billy, throwing wild punches and cursing at him. It had taken four guys to separate Jeff from Billy, and both still bore some animosity toward each other.

From his body language, Matt sensed that Billy was about to withdraw his agreement and would fly the demo himself. So,

Matt quickly walked up behind Jeff and put his hand on his shoulder.

The change in Jeff's tone when he felt Matt's touch was immediate; all his rage instantly dissipated. Matt then said,

"The plane checks out great. Thanks for giving me a chance to fly her, Billy."

Matt then promised to put on a good show. But if he experienced any problems, he wanted Billy's permission to fly the plane to another airport close by, where Matt's former chief mechanic, Wes Potts, ran a fixed-based shop. He would have the plane more thoroughly inspected and repaired, if necessary, before Billy tried to fly the plane home.

Billy, under Jeff's mostly-subdued glare, agreed to Matt's conditions.

It was now 11:30 am, close to the time negotiated by Billy with the air traffic control tower for the 15-minute air show to begin. Matt asked Billy to watch the show from the Control Tower, but Billy mentioned that he had a radio scanner that he could use to listen to Matt's communication with the controller. Matt, though, said he wanted Billy to watch from the tower in case he needed to speak with him.

As soon as Billy left, Jeff grabbed Matt and pleaded with him not to fly. Jeff didn't have a good feeling, probably just because it was Billy's plane, and everything that Billy touched seemed to turn to crap.

But Matt said he'd be fine and not to worry. They'd all been extra careful with the pre-flight inspection. In fact, it had been the most thorough pre-flight check Matt had ever given. But Matt also admitted that, selfishly, he wanted one last chance to fly a P-38. When would he ever get another?

Jeff helped Matt put on his flight suit, then his parachute, carefully checking that the straps weren't tangled and that all the clips were fastened correctly.

Matt was just about to step up on the boarding ladder when Jeff reached to embrace him, saying,

"Promise me that at the first sign of trouble, you'll bail out of this crate.

"And no fancy aerobatics, OK? No one's paying to see this show, you know. There will be three people at the most in the stands."

Matt just nodded his head and gave his usual reassuring reply,

"No worries. I'll be back before you know it."

Matt climbed the boarding ladder, lowered from the rear of the gondola, walked up the port-side wing root, and was helped into the cockpit by the mechanic who had helped with the inspection earlier.

The mechanic helped close the cockpit canopy and, smiling warmly, gave Matt a thumbs-up before climbing down from the plane and stowing the boarding ladder.

He'd noticed earlier Matt subtly massaging the back of Jeff's neck with his thumb when his hand was on Jeff's shoulder and the immediate calming effect it had had on Jeff. It reminded him how much he missed his friend, Josh, also a mechanic, who had served with him in Korea, and who had been killed when he had been sucked into the inlet of an F-86A Sabre jet engine. He and Josh had just turned nineteen less than a week before.

#

AIRSHOW

Matt was always meticulous in his flight preparations, but this flight felt a little unplanned. So, as he waited on the tarmac for the engines to warm up again, he worked on his flight plan.

He'd start with just a simple take-off, gently climb to about 5000 feet, and see how the plane handled. If, after a few slow banks and turns, everything seemed OK, he'd try a fly-by at about 1500 feet. If all went well, he'd get a little more aerobatic and finish with a zoom-climb - a high-speed, low-level fly-by at about 500 feet, ending with a steep, nearly vertical climb - before landing.

The purpose of the flight, though, besides keeping Billy on the ground, was to stress-test the plane. He didn't plan to cover the full-combat flight envelope, but he did intend to stress the plane enough to be sure that Billy wouldn't experience any trouble flying home.

At noon exactly, Matt radioed the Control Tower and asked for permission to taxi to the runway. The Control Tower had just shut the field down for the show, so no other planes were taxiing or in the landing pattern.

The Control Tower quickly gave permission, and Matt taxied to the head of the runway. When positioned, Matt ran one final power check of the engines, then radioed the tower for clearance to take off. The Control Tower gave him clearance, then wished him good luck.

Matt pushed both throttles forward to take off rpm, and the P-38 began to race down the runway. At less than 1500 feet, the plane reached V-1 speed, Matt pulled back slightly on the yoke, and the plane leaped into the air. Matt then adjusted the controls for a rate of climb of 1000 feet a minute.

Despite Jeff's prediction, the 200-seat grandstands along the taxiway were nearly packed. When Matt hit the throttles, the engine roar was deafening, and many in the crowd covered their ears as the plane roared by.

Jeff was watching from the chain-link fence at the end of the taxiway, close to where the plane lifted off. Mike and Linda were in the grandstands.

The climb to 5000 feet was uneventful, as were the slow banks and turns that Matt put the plane through as a preliminary stress test and for him to get the feel of the plane. It had been almost 16 years since he'd last flown a P-38, and he had forgotten just how responsive the controls were. The passenger jets he was now flying were lumbering giants in comparison and, ignoring the awful purpose the P-38 was designed for, the plane was a joy to fly.

Thomas Willard © 2023

Now that he had the feel of the plane, he thought he'd try some loops over the field, nothing producing too many G's or getting too close to the ground. He did several of those and a figure-8 and thought that that was enough; he'd next go for the high-speed, low-altitude fly-by, with a quick near-vertical climb for a finale, and then land.

He moved to the approach circle's outer perimeter while reducing his altitude to 500 feet. Then, when the plane was lined with the runway, he pushed the throttles to full power.

The plane quickly accelerated from 150 mph to 250 mph, and just as he passed the grandstands, he pulled back on the yoke, and the plane started a nearly vertical climb.

But at the same instant that he'd pulled back on the yoke, he heard a loud bang, so he immediately pushed the yoke forward to reduce the G level and the rate of climb.

He wasn't sure where the noise had come from and didn't feel any difference in the controls but sensed something was

Thomas Willard © 2023

wrong. Maybe some foreign object (FOB) was rolling around that could jam the controls, or worse, something had failed structurally.

Jeff was still at the fence, near the point where Matt had started his vertical climb. He noticed right away that Matt had backed off the climb early, well before Jeff had expected he would. Though he didn't see anything fall from the plane or hear anything odd, he sensed there was something wrong and started making his way to the Control Tower.

Matt leveled off at 2500 feet, called the tower to thank them, and to let them know that the show was over. But he didn't mention any problems.

He asked the tower to tell Billy that he was enjoying the flight so much that he was taking the plane for a little joy ride and hoped that Billy wouldn't mind. He also requested Billy let Jeff know that he would be late for dinner, that they should go on without him, and that he'd be seeing him, so no worries. Then, Matt signed off and exited the field's controlled-airspace.

#

Thomas Willard © 2023

NO WORRIES

Jeff reached the tower just as Matt had signed off and quickly asked Billy what was going on. Billy, still a little miffed at Jeff from the morning's confrontation and now even more put out by Matt "stealing" his pride and joy, was slow to respond. So, Jeff asked the controller what had happened.

The controller said everything was normal, with no report of any problems, but that Matt had had such a great time flying the plane that he wanted to borrow it for a while longer. Matt had asked Billy to give Jeff a message that he would be late for dinner, so they should go on without him, and that his final words were "he'd be seeing him" and "no worries."

Jeff asked the controller to repeat the message as closely word-for-word as he could. When the controller said he had written it all down, then read back the message from his notes, the message was the same. By this time, Billy was over his anger and confirmed the message, word-for-word.

Thomas Willard © 2023

Jeff then asked the controller for Matt's heading when he exited the control space and what airports were on that heading. The controller said the heading was on a direct line to the Santa Maria airport, about 25 miles to the southeast.

Jeff thanked the controller and was about to leave when he remembered that Billy had mentioned he had a portable radio scanner in his car that could receive air traffic control channels.

Trying to get on Billy's good side, Jeff apologized for his earlier confrontation. He said he'd been way out of line, probably just jealous of Billy's new plane. Jeff then begged to borrow Billy's radio. Billy, though, was in no mood to lend Jeff anything and refused, though given a few minutes, he would have relented and given Jeff anything that he asked for; next to Matt, he admired Jeff the most and always wished that they'd been closer. If anyone was jealous, it was Billy over Jeff and Matt's close friendship.

The controller, who had listened to Jeff practically debase himself, now thought that something was up. He pulled his own portable scanner from a desk drawer and, handing it to Jeff, said,

"Here, take this. I don't care when you bring it back. I just hope everything is OK. Please let me know if there is anything else I can do to help."

Jeff quickly thanked the controller again, shaking his hand, and promised to let him know how things were going. Then, he swung down the stairs of the tower, two at a time using the railings, and raced as fast as he could for his car, which was parked in the lot behind the grandstands.

#

CHAPTER 5 — 15TH YEAR REUNION: DAY TWO: EARLY AFTERNOON

THE CHASE

Linda and Mike were just exiting the bleachers when they spotted Jeff making a beeline for the parking lot. They yelled his name, catching his attention, but he tried to hand-gesture that he had to go, mouthed the word "urgent," and then gestured that he'd call.

Mike picked up on the word "urgent" and told his mother he was going with his dad. Linda said to be careful and for them to call her at the hotel as soon as they could.

Jeff was just backing out of his parking spot when Mike reached the passenger's side door. Jeff stopped to let Mike in but said he needed to go somewhere fast and that Mike should go and tell his mother that he'd call her at the hotel as soon as he could.

Mike was now worried and asked Jeff what was wrong and if he could go with him.

Jeff stopped then to consider what was best for Mike: to leave him worrying about some unknown danger or to tell him what he thought might be happening. He looked at Mike, saw the real concern on his face, and opted to tell him the truth.

He told Mike that he could come along, that he could use his company. And then he started to explain, saying,

"I'm not sure, but Matt may be in trouble. I think I know where he's headed, and I want to be there in case something goes wrong.

"If there's a chance it's going to end badly, though, I don't want you to watch - Matt wouldn't want that either - so you have to promise me that you'll look away if I ask you to."

Thomas Willard © 2023

Mike, choked up and reeling from the news, could barely answer. "I promise, Dad."

Then Jeff asked Mike to turn on the scanner so they could listen to any communication Matt had with the Santa Maria Control Tower.

#

THE TALK

Once Matt left the San Luis Obispo airspace, he contacted the Santa Maria tower.

"Santa Maria Tower, this is Lockheed N5753, ten miles to the north-northwest at 2500 feet, inbound to Santa Maria."

"Lockheed N5753, this is Santa Maria Tower. We have you on our radar. Over."

"I have an emergency. I may have a structural problem that could affect landing. Over."

"Copy, Lockheed N5743. Do you need emergency clearance to land now?"

"Negative. I have about 3 hours of fuel remaining and would like to circle your perimeter to burn the fuel off."

"Copy, you're clear to circle the perimeter as long as you need. We'll vector other traffic away from you. Let us know if your condition changes and you need emergency landing clearance. We'll notify the Emergency Rescue crew now of your condition and approximate landing time."

"Copy, Santa Maria Tower. I'll contact you when I'm ready to land or if my condition suddenly changes. Over."

"Copy, Lockheed N5743. Good luck. Out."

Once the communication with the tower was over, Matt switched radio frequencies to the airport's only aircraft maintenance facility, Coastal Valley Aviation, owned by Wes Potts, Matt's former chief line mechanic while they were stationed at Nuthampstead and Wormingford airfields with the 55th Fighter Group in England.

The ground crews were the unsung heroes of WWII, working grueling hours in often crude conditions, exposed to the weather and hazards of war, keeping complex aircraft flying with a limited supply of spare parts, often having to jury-rig, using spit and wire, and cannibalizing damaged aircraft.

Formal USAAF tech school training of aircraft mechanics in WWII was surprisingly extensive, lasting over nine months, and included time on the production line at the aircraft manufacturer's factory.

Still, it relied heavily on on-the-job training by the more senior mechanics. Through experience and innate mechanical ability, some of the chief mechanics eventually knew as much about the planes they serviced as the aircraft designers, at least from a technician's level. And Wes Potts was one of the best chief mechanics on the P-38 in the USAAF.

Matt was just a sergeant pilot when he first met Wes, so he was able to get close without any concerns over fraternizing. Wes had noticed Matt was a loner, not fitting in with the slightly older officer pilots, and enjoyed getting his hands dirty. So, Wes had befriended him and taught him the mechanics of the P-38 from the inside out.

"Coastal Valley Aviation, this is Lockheed N5743. Over."

"Lockheed N5743, this is Coastal Valley Aviation. Over."

"Yes, this is Matt Yetman. Is Wes Potts handy? Over."

"Hi, Matt, this is Wes. Good to hear your voice again after so long. Over."

"Hi, Wes. Good to hear you, too.

"Sorry to drop in on you like this, but I'm circling your field in an old P-38 that Billy Dempsey brought to the reunion, and I have a problem that I need your help with. Over."

"Ouch, Billy strikes again. Matt, I'll help you in any way that I can. What do you think the problem is? Over."

Matt described to Wes the extensive pre-flight inspection and then what had happened during the demonstration, the loud bang he'd heard with the high-G zoom-climb maneuver. Wes took a moment to consider what he'd been told and then had a few questions.

"Matt, have you noticed any change in the controls, like buffeting or the need to increase trim or power to maintain flight altitude and airspeed? Over"

"I haven't noticed any change in the controls or power requirements. Over."

"You mentioned the noise was a loud bang just below and behind you. Do you remember what side it was on, left or right? Over."

"I don't remember what side it was on. Over."

"Do you remember what direction you turned your head? Over."

"Thanks, that did help me remember. I turned my head to the left so the noise came from the port side. Over."

"Ok, I'll look from the ground with my binoculars the next time you fly over the field to see if I can spot anything that doesn't look right. But I think I'll need to come up in a chase plane to spot anything small, like a missing inspection panel.

Thomas Willard © 2023

"A nose panel flying off and hitting the rear of the fuselage could have made a loud bang from where you heard it, but you'd think any missing panels would be felt in the controls.

"A FOB rolling around is pretty scary: it could jam the controls at any time. But the FOB would have to be large to make the kind of sound you heard, and someone would have had to have been seriously negligent to leave a FOB that large in the plane. Over."

"Wes, I agree that it's probably not a FOB or a missing inspection panel. I'd appreciate it if you could get someone to fly you up to look, though, just to eliminate that possibility.

"I know you don't like considering this, but that leaves a structural failure. Any idea of what might have let go? Over."

"Matt, I'm just guessing, but I think it's the inner wing-to-gondola joint. The outer and inner wing-to-nacelle joints are too far away, and so are the nacelle-to-boom joints: the sound would have been more outboard, and you'd have noticed that. The same for anything rattling around in the main landing gear bay. Over."

Thomas Willard © 2023

"Wes, I think you are right. If it's not the joint itself, it's one of the wing spars or ribs near it. Over."

"That's why I wanted to know which side the sound was on. Over."

"This isn't a fair question, Wes, but do you have any recommendations? Over."

"I know you don't want to lose the plane, Matt, but my only concern is for you. Santa Maria's Class D airspace, with its 4.5-nautical mile radius circular path, will bring you over mostly unpopulated farmland where you could bail out or make an emergency landing if you had to. Over."

"Thanks, Wes. You know it's not easy to bail out of one of these planes, and there are not that many P-38s left in flying condition, so I'd kind of like to bring this one back. Plus, Billy will kill me if I wreck his plane. Over."

"I'd trade the plane for you in a second, but you're right; it's not an easy decision. If I had to, I'd put my life in the hands of you and Kelly Johnson and not lose any sleep over it.

"You're the best P-38 pilot I've ever known, flying the best plane, for my money, that ever flew, designed by the best aeronautical engineer there ever was.

"You've seen the guts of a P-38, so you know. They are way overbuilt, which is probably why you're still in the air. Over."

"Wow, me and Kelly Johnson mentioned in the same breath. My face is burning. Thanks, Wes, you've helped me make up my mind. But no matter how things turn out, remember I made the final decision on my own; you had nothing to do with it.

"Ok, so unless something suddenly changes for the worse, I plan to land at Santa Maria in about three hours, around 4:00 pm. Over."

"We'll check from the ground first, but I have a buddy with a Cessna 172 that I can get to take me up to have a closer look in about 20 minutes, but I don't expect to find anything.

"If we don't, there are a couple of things that might help reduce the risk of complete joint failure on landing, assuming we've identified the problem correctly.

Thomas Willard © 2023

"I think you should use minimum flaps, land on the starboard-side main gear first, and avoid braking at high speed, all to reduce the landing load on the port-side wing-to-fuselage joint. You might even consider feathering the port engine before landing, so in case the joint fails, you won't be in any danger of shrapnel from the rotating prop hitting the ground. Over."

"That sounds good. Maybe there will be a headwind when I land, and I won't need a lot of flaps or braking. Thanks a lot for your advice. I guess I'll see you and your friend in a little bit. Out."

Jeff and Mike had listened to Matt's conversations with the tower and Wes Potts. Jeff thought Matt had seemed calm, but then Matt always did in emergencies. Still, Jeff judged that Matt didn't think he was in any immediate danger. And at least Jeff knew for sure where Matt was headed.

They had been driving for about 30 minutes and were nearing the entrance to the Santa Maria airport when Mike noticed the sign on the Coastal Valley Aviation hangar. Jeff pulled into the hangar's graveled parking lot and recognized Wes Potts, Matt's

Thomas Willard © 2023

former crew chief, standing in front of the hangar, looking skyward through a pair of binoculars.

Jeff and Mike walked towards Wes, who lowered his binoculars when he heard them approaching from the sound of crunching gravel. Reaching out to shake their hands, Wes said,

"Hi, Jeff. Good to see you. This must be Mike."

After their greeting, Jeff let Wes know he understood the situation: they'd heard all of Matt's exchanges with the tower and with Wes and knew that Wes was about to go up to take a closer look at Matt's plane.

Wes said, "I'll be gone for a couple of hours.

"It'll take an hour or so to inspect the '38 from the air. I don't expect to find anything, though. Once I get back down, I'll stop at the tower to give them an update and then visit the Emergency Rescue crew. They're all good men, a lot of ex-military. Matt's in good hands.

"It's getting pretty hot out here. You can wait in the hangar; it's air-conditioned.

"I've just finished restoring a '51 that you're welcome to check out, or you can camp out in my office, the first door to the left just inside.

"You probably haven't eaten yet. I'll ask one of my mechanics, Al, to round you up some sandwiches and sodas from the airport café before I leave."

Wes, seeing the concern on Jeff and Mike's faces, placed his hand on Jeff's shoulder and then added,

"Matt is a great pilot, the same as you. He's always using this irritating saying he picked up from the Aussie pilots in England, "No worries." For once, I think we should listen to him."

Then Wes walked to meet a mechanic just passing through the half-opened hangar doors, spoke to him for a moment, then waved back to Jeff and Mike as he left to meet his friend with the Cessna.

Jeff and Mike walked inside the hangar and were shown to Wes' office by the mechanic. On the walls were photographs of planes restored by Wes, along with Wes' family.

Thomas Willard © 2023

A few were from his WWII days in England, of members of his line crew, and at the center was one of Matt. But there was another one, of Matt and Jeff, both with beaming smiles and with Jeff's arm over Matt's shoulder, pulling him into an embrace. Written on the photo was an inscription,

"Wes, I took your advice and trusted him. You were so right. I can't thank you enough. Forever, Matt."

When Jeff saw the photo of him and Matt and read the inscription, he started to tear up. Mike noticed and read the inscription himself, finally reaching a breaking point.

He'd been trying to make sense of Matt's relationship with his dad and mom - their extreme affection for one another. They obviously loved each other, but Mike could not make sense of the boundaries of their relationship. Did Matt really desire his mom, and if he did, why would his dad put up with it, even worship Matt for it?

Mike loved Matt as well and was full of concern right then for his safety. But something was off. There were too many secrets. He was confused and hurt that no one would trust him to tell him the truth. Even his dad's Squadron members seemed to know more than he did: he'd overheard them discussing a secret agreement they called "the arrangement," swearing them not to disclose anything about Jeff and Matt's relationship.

So, Mike resolved to ask his dad to come clean.

"Dad, what's going on between you, Mom, and Uncle Matt? I'm old enough to know. You need to tell me."

Jeff was at first taken aback by Mike's question. But he'd been trying to think of a way to explain things to Mike for a while, and this seemed like as good a time as any.

"Mike, you're right; you are old and mature enough now to know. I was going to tell you soon anyway. It all goes back to WWII when we were both stationed in England, but it also includes our tour in Korea and the times in between the wars and after, including up until today.

"Let me tell you the whole story all the way through before you ask me any questions; I may not get through it all without breaking down otherwise. Then I'll try to answer any questions that you have.

"I'll tell you everything that I know, but Matt is a little cagy and hasn't told me everything that happened. Wes and I know things that Matt doesn't – some things that happened in the ambulance when Matt was unconscious and nearly died - but we thought it best not to tell him.

"I haven't told your mother half of what I'm about to tell you, and probably never will: it would only upset her to learn how many times Matt and I came so close to dying. There's a psychiatrist in Boston, though, that's smarter than Matt, Wes, and I put together, and I'm sure he knows everything, at least about what happened in England.

"This story is almost unbelievable – I lived through it and still don't believe it – and involves acts of bravery, incredible flying skill, and even insubordination on Matt's part – I wouldn't be here, and neither would you or your sister otherwise – of his refusing the Congressional Medal of Honor, our multiple near-death experiences, of both of us suffering unbearable emotional and physical pain, of learning to swim, dance, and sail from each other, and of a wingman's responsibility and loyalty to his flight leader and friend. But mostly, it's about caring more for someone else's life than your own.

"In the end, at least for me, it just comes down to love – its many different types - and how it can come at you from multiple and surprising directions. I've been very lucky in love, experiencing it in stereo from two extraordinary people. I don't think anyone has ever been luckier.

"It's a lot to take in, I know, but I think you're up to it; at least, I'm betting that you are."

Jeff motioned for Mike to sit in Wes' desk chair while he stood, braced by the desk, looking out of the office window at the flight line. Then, in a flat, matter-of-fact voice, he began recalling the details of his and Matt's amazing journey together as each other's adopted and blood brother, best friend, and lover in so many ways, but most importantly, as each other's wingman.

Thomas Willard © 2023

With his back to the door, Jeff hadn't noticed someone else

enter Wes' office and was now raptly listening to Jeff's talk with

Mike.

#

CHAPTER 6 — 15TH YEAR REUNION: DAY TWO: LATE AFTERNOON

LANDING

As soon as Jeff had left the San Luis Obispo's Control Tower, Billy realized that something was wrong and tried to follow Jeff. But Jeff had been too quick and had driven from the parking lot before Billy even reached his car.

Using the same reasoning as Jeff to track Matt, Billy turned his portable scanner on and listened to Matt's communications with Santa Maria's Control Tower and with Wes at Coastal Valley

Aviation, and arrived at Wes' office about ten minutes after Jeff and Mike, just as Jeff began to relate his and Matt's story to Mike.

It took Jeff about two hours to complete the tale. About halfway through, he'd turned and noticed Billy in the doorway listening but continued anyway, thinking Billy had probably already heard the most intimate details of their history, so why worry about him hearing the rest?

Just as Jeff was beginning to wrap up, Wes returned from his observation flight and, sensing what Jeff was doing, waited to let him finish.

As soon as Jeff was through, Mike, with tears pouring down his face, grabbed Jeff and, unable to speak, just hugged him and sobbed while Jeff tried to comfort him by stroking his hair.

Seeing that Billy was crying too, Jeff motioned for him to join Mike, and the three held each other for several minutes while Wes quietly left the room to give them some privacy.

When Wes returned, he found the three just separating, and without acknowledging their emotional state, matter-of-factly reported that he and the pilot of the chase plane hadn't seen anything obviously wrong - like a missing inspection panel - with the P-38.

Then Wes said that Matt was going to land in a few minutes. But when he looked at Jeff, Mike, and Billy and suggested they head out to the runway to watch, he found three terrified faces staring back.

Realizing how afraid they were for Matt, Wes, with as confident a voice as he could muster but without any false bravado, said,

"Hey, guys, what's this?

"Jeff, you know Matt's one of the best P-38 pilots there ever was, the same as you. And you've both been in much worse situations than this one."

Then looking at Mike, Wes said,

"Your dad's always been hyper-protective of Matt; he can't help it. But Matt's an amazing pilot, and I'm sure he'll land this plane safely, no worries. So, come on, let's go see how it's done," getting a nod from Jeff in agreement.

When they arrived mid-way along the side of the main runway, they could see the P-38 lined up with the runway about one mile away and at 1000 feet elevation. Matt had feathered the port engine, lowered the landing gear and flaps – there was little headwind - and turned on the landing lights to make the plane more visible to the tower. They could also see the Emergency Rescue crew stationed near the runway at the ready: Matt had requested emergency landing clearance, and the Control Tower had shut down the rest of the airfield.

Matt idled the engine and lowered his airspeed to 110 mph just as he passed over the imaginary fence 100 feet before the beginning of the runway.

As he pulled back on the yoke and started to flare, with the nose high, he dipped the right wing, so the right main landing gear would make contact with the runway first. He balanced there briefly before leveling the plane, contacting the runway with the left main gear, quickly followed by the nose gear.

The instant the left main landing gear tire contacted the runway, Matt heard a loud bang to his left and then noticed a slight sag in the gondola to port.

He kept the plane centered using the control surfaces, avoiding braking until his indicated airspeed fell below 55 mph.

As he slowed, he radioed the Control Tower to thank them, then taxied to the front of the Coastal Valley Aviation hangar using a combination of starboard-engine power and braking before moving the engine's mixture control to Idle Cut-off and the magneto switch to Off, shutting the engine down.

#

WET WELCOME AND A LITTLE HORSE TRADING

Matt waited in the cockpit until one of Wes' mechanics had chocked the tires. He expected to find Wes there to greet him, but when he opened the canopy and started to climb out, assisted by the mechanic, he was shocked to find Jeff, Mike, and Billy there, as well as Wes, just returning from the runway.

As soon as he'd climbed down from the gondola's ladder, Matt was greeted by a stoic but still nervous Wes and Jeff, and a sheepish Billy, who each shook his hand, and then by a tearful Mike, who wrapped his arms around him and was unabashedly sobbing, saying how sorry he was for giving him a hard time before, and how glad he was that Matt was safe.

Matt held Mike for a moment to let him calm down, then released him, saying,

"That emergency wasn't so bad. The Tower was great, and Wes diagnosed the problem perfectly.

"See, they've already reopened the field," as he pointed to planes taking off and landing again.

Then, looking at Billy, Matt said,

"Thanks, Billy, for letting me take her up. She's a beauty except for the joint problem. I hope Wes will be able to fix her up again soon."

Thomas Willard © 2023

Before Billy could answer, Mike, still frightened and hurting, said,

"I hate that plane; it's a piece of junk."

Matt, now fully appreciating just how upset Mike was and suddenly noticing how quiet Billy and Jeff had been, said,

"No, you don't mean that. The P-38 is my favorite plane of all time. Tell him, guys, how great a plane the Lightning is."

When Matt got no response, Wes, trying to lighten the mood, pointed to the newly restored P-51 visible through the opened doors of the hanger and said,

"When you get a chance, Mike, take a look at the Mustang; you may like it better. But both the P-38 and the P-51 were great planes in their day. Your dad, Matt, and Billy flew both of those planes during the war and battled against the most advanced fighters the Germans had, including jets. Those two planes won the air war over Europe and racked up a combined kill ratio of 8:1, bringing most of their pilots back home safely."

Thomas Willard © 2023

Then Matt suddenly thought of a plan that would help save Billy from financial disaster with the P-38, get him to switch to a plane that he was more suited to fly - the P-51 - and, if things worked out, might even get Jeff back into the cockpit. Matt started,

"Wes, I can see from here how great a job you've done restoring the Mustang. Would you be interested in doing a little horse trading with me and my new airplane partner here, Billy? I'm buying a half-interest in his '38.

"We don't want any special discounts, so we'll need to see something in writing, like an ad or listing somewhere, that shows your current asking price.

"As a separate deal, we'd like you to give us an estimate on what it would cost to repair the '38, your opinion of whether it would be better to repair the plane or to sell it for parts, what you think it would cost to restore the plane, and how much you think it would be worth afterward. We'll go along with whatever you recommend, won't we, Billy?" getting a nod from a flabbergasted Billy in return.

An equally astonished Jeff took a moment but quickly caught on to what Matt was up to and said,

"Hey, I want in on this deal, too," getting a broad, knowing smile from Matt, who said,

"OK, you and I will split a half-partnership."

Wes, savvier than Matt, Jeff, and Billy put together when it came to horse-trading, said, "Don't you think you should take a look at the Mustang first, maybe give it a test flight, before getting too carried away?"

Matt, grinning, said, "Yep, you're right. Billy and I will check out the plane with you, and then Billy will give it a test flight before we talk turkey."

Then while looking at Jeff, Matt, in a gentle, encouraging voice, said,

"While Billy and I are looking at the '51, why don't you take Mike up to the cockpit of the '38 and give him a tour? Let him sit in the pilot's seat and help him start the starboard engine; I'm sure you still remember how," getting an enthusiastic, "Yeah, Dad!" from Mike and a slightly frightened but resigned, "Ok, that sounds good," from Jeff, who then thought, "Linda's going to kill us both when she finds out."

#

NO MORE HIDING

After Jeff gave Mike a tour of the P-38 and guided him through starting and stopping the engine, they joined Matt, Wes, and Billy at the Mustang.

A much more excited Mike asked to sit in the cockpit of the P-51, and Jeff helped him in and then gave him a tour of the instrument panel and the flight and engine controls.

When it was time to roll the Mustang out of the hanger for Billy to give it a flight test, Matt and Jeff decided Billy could handle the rest of the negotiations without them, and they and Mike left for the ride back to San Luis Obispo.

Thomas Willard © 2023

When they got to the car, Jeff climbed into the driver's side of the four-door sedan and Matt into the passenger's side, but they were immediately joined up front by Mike, who squeezed Matt into the middle of the bench seat. Matt thought it strange because Mike would normally be sprawled out on the back seat trying to get some sleep. But when Mike put his arm around his shoulder, Matt knew for certain something was off and asked,

"OK, something's up. What am I missing?"

Jeff took a deep breath, then answered,

"Mike and I talked while you were up there. He asked me about your, my, and Linda's relationship, and I told him everything."

Stunned, Matt asked Jeff, "Everything, everything?"

But Mike answered for Jeff, saying, "Yes, everything, everything," before squeezing Matt's shoulder.

Jeff said, "He thought you were hitting on Linda last night. That's why he was so angry at you."

Thomas Willard © 2023

Matt, still reeling, said, "He was mad when he thought I was hitting on Linda, but he's OK with me hitting on you?"

Mike again answered for Jeff, saying, "Yes, because you're each other's "Forever Wingman." I can see the MIT rings on your fingers and know what they mean."

Then Mike added, "The only thing that will upset me is if you hide your affection for each other from me anymore.

"Dad is hurting from worrying about you all day, and the only thing that will help him is for you to hold him. But you won't because I'm here."

Mike, crying a little now, said, "Please, Uncle Matt, he needs you. Just put your arm around him like mine is around you."

Matt slowly lifted his arm and wrapped it around Jeff. Then Mike said,

"Thanks, that's good. Everything's even now, just the way the three of us like it. Now promise me, no more hiding, ever again," getting a nod in agreement from both Matt and Jeff.

Thomas Willard © 2023

As they were pulling into the hotel's parking lot, Mike asked Matt for a favor.

"Uncle Matt, I know you're not a blood relative, so you are not really my uncle. But I'm glad of that because addressing you as uncle is now getting in the way of me being closer to you. If it's OK with you, from now on, I'd like to call you Matt like my mom and dad or any of your close friends do."

Matt said he'd be honored if Mike considered him a close friend and that Mike could drop the uncle title and call him by his first name.

A beaming Mike thanked Matt and then, once Jeff was out of earshot, secretly asked Matt for one more favor.

#

CHAPTER 7 — 15TH YEAR REUNION: DAY TWO

EVENING: IT'S ABOUT TIME

THE HERMIT'S ANNOUNCEMENTS

Colonel Crowell waited for the first record to finish playing, Tony

Pastor's "Just for Kicks," before addressing the crowd.

"Can I have your attention, please? Before we continue

with the dance portion of the evening, I've been asked to make a

few announcements on behalf of someone calling himself "The

Hermit."

"The Hermit" thanks you more than he can say for abiding

by the terms of "the arrangement" all these years. He's always considered that a sign of your deep affection for him. But he wants me to announce that, after today's events, "the arrangement" is no longer needed, so it is now and forever canceled, and all its terms are no longer in effect.

"About time, I'd say.

"Per his first announcement, all drinks for the remainder of the evening will be on him, in partial payback for all the times he was unable to return the favor. He says beer never was so warm but tasted as good as it did back then in England.

"He wishes all of you a safe trip home and looks forward to seeing you again at next year's reunion.

"By the way, he's bribed me with my favorite cocktail to play three songs by request next, so please, let's indulge him. I bet at least one of you will find special meaning in two of his selections.

"And ladies, rumor has it that he's partial to Dinah Washington and can't refuse an invitation to dance to any of her songs, so when you hear one start, you might want to grab him.

He's already chosen someone for his first song, though."

#

YOU TAUGHT HIM THE CODE?

Matt, aka "The Hermit," knew that an enthused Mike had by now

told Linda about his sitting in the cockpit of two fighter planes,

even getting to start one up, and that Matt and Jeff had bought a

Mustang, all in violation of the oath he and Jeff had sworn to Linda

not to expose Mike to the allure of flying, at least not until he was

eighteen.

So, he came up with a plan to try and get back in Linda's

good graces, bribing Colonel Crowell to play three songs for him.

When the first song started, Dinah Washington's "Don't

Go to Strangers," Matt sheepishly approached an obviously furious

Linda and asked her to dance. Linda, who was angry, but more

from fear and worrying herself sick all afternoon about Matt – she hated anything to do with flying now more than ever - relented and let Matt lead her onto the dance floor.

Once they started to dance, Matt sensed Linda's anger melt away and said,

"I'm sorry; I know I promised not to ever let Mike get close to an airplane, but things just happened."

"I don't think you have anything to worry about, though; you've had more influence on him than Jeff and me. He's not going to run off to the Air Force Academy to become a fighter pilot. He wants to be a doctor and has his hopes set on getting into Harvard.

"Like most guys, he gets excited around planes and flying. But with Mike, I think it's mostly about getting closer to his dad than an obsession for flying."

Linda kissed Matt on the cheek, then said,

"I wasn't really angry with you. I was just scared again; you can tell I hate flying. I know it's a little irrational, but you can't blame me after all the times I've come so close to losing one or both of you."

Matt said, "I'm sorry for all that I put you through today. The last two songs I requested are for you and have some surprises. I hope they make up for things a little."

When the song ended, as Matt led Linda back to Jeff, Linda said,

"Thanks, Matt, for the dance and your two surprises; I'm sure I'll enjoy them both," then, with a Cheshire cat smile, she added, "I have a surprise for you, too, but I'll give it to you later."

No sooner had Linda and Matt returned to Jeff than the next song started, Frank Sinatra's 1959s upbeat version of his 1940s hit, "I'll Be Seeing You."

Linda, knowing the song was meant for her, looked around but only saw Matt, Jeff, and Mike near her. When she looked at Matt and Jeff, they both shrugged. But then a smiling Mike took Linda's hand and led her out to the center of the dance floor.

Thomas Willard © 2023

The second favor Mike had asked Matt for when they'd returned to the hotel was for Matt to teach him how to dance, at least enough so that he could dance one song with his mom later that night. Matt and Mike had spent the next two hours rehearsing in the hotel's ballroom, with Matt teaching Mike the first three moves from his and Jeff's dance code. Just like Jeff when Matt had danced with Linda, Matt would provide Mike hand signals in real-time from the sidelines to choreograph the steps.

Matt raised three fingers, and Mike started dancing with Linda, using the third step.

An astonished Jeff, who was unaware of Matt and Mike's plan, wildly exclaimed,

"You taught him the code!" which caused both Matt and Jeff to burst into laughter.

Matt was laughing so hard he was doubled over and couldn't even raise his fingers to guide Mike.

A frustrated and now disgusted Mike soon stopped dancing. But Linda, seeing what was happening, pointed two fingers at her eyes, indicating for Mike to look at her, then held one finger up, signaling that Mike should switch to the first step in the code.

Matt and Jeff, still hysterically laughing and with an arm draped over each other's shoulder for support, like two drunken sailors, watched the exchange between Mike and Linda from the sidelines and together incredulously said,

"She knows the code!" triggering another fit of laughter from them both.

When an exuberant Linda and a slightly miffed Mike returned to Matt and Jeff, Linda kissed all three on the cheek, showing that she was well over any anger she had about that afternoon.

But Matt wasn't through with her yet.

As the next song began, Harry James' version of "It's Been a Long Time," Matt looked at Jeff and tenderly said, "It's your turn, big guy."

Thomas Willard © 2023

Seeing the terror on Jeff's face from his fear of stumbling, Matt whispered in Jeff's ear,

"Just place your right hand on Linda's shoulder and bear down a little to steady yourself. You do that dancing with me all the time, and you've never had a problem."

Then, when Jeff still hadn't moved to take Linda's hand, Matt added this.

"When I was terrified in Romsey, you told me slow dancing wasn't about fancy footwork; it was all about body contact.

"She's danced with me enough. Make her day and give her the real thing. It's about time."

At that, Jeff took Linda's hand and walked her out onto the dance floor. Jeff steadied himself with his right hand on Linda's shoulder, then wrapped his left arm around her waist, pulling her in close, and started to dance.

Thomas Willard © 2023

Almost instantly, Jeff's fears melted away, and he pulled a now sobbing Linda in even closer. Then they kissed passionately, not caring who was watching.

Just then, Matt felt a tap on his shoulder and turned to find a smiling Wes standing next to him.

Matt said, "Hey, Wes. Glad to see you. Did you bring your wife along?"

Wes said, "No, Billy flew the Mustang here, and I'm just returning his car. My eldest son, John, is here with my middle daughter, Nancy. They followed me here in my car, so I have a way to get home."

When Matt looked around to try and find Mike, he saw that Mike had already noticed Nancy, or the other way around, and had asked her to dance.

"Wes, I hope you're not upset, but it looks like Mike might be interested in Nancy, at least in her dancing. He's a good guy, though, so no worries."

Thomas Willard © 2023

Wes, smiling, said, "She noticed Mike dancing with his mom when we first got here, and I think she's a little smitten with him. I know he's a good guy – he'd have to be with Jeff for a dad - so she could do a lot worse. Besides, her six-foot-four, 225-pound brother is keeping a pretty close eye on them."

When Wes caught Matt wistfully staring at Linda and Jeff dancing, he said,

"You know, you've always had it backward. You're sharing him with her and are the one that's being generous. She knows that and is grateful to you. Never feel guilty about loving him.

"And as far as Jeff loving you, you didn't see how distraught he was today while you were circling the field or hear his talk with Mike. I only caught the tail end of it, but it brought both Mike and Billy to tears."

Jeff and Linda stayed on the dance floor as the next song started, Tony Bennett's "I Wanna Be Around." Wes, with a devilish grin, said, "I requested this one. Come on, dance with me.

Thomas Willard © 2023

I've always wanted the chance to hold you," as he led a startled Matt onto the dance floor.

As they began to dance, Wes asked, "So how come we never got together back in England?"

Matt, knowing he was being teased, said, "Ah, maybe it was the dozen kids you had that gave me a clue you wouldn't be interested."

Smiling, Wes said, "I only had three at the time," then added,

"You know I've always loved you, right? Maybe not in all the ways that Jeff does. But I've always wanted to at least hold you.

"Look around the room. There are about 125 other guys here that would all say the same thing, and some, like Billy – hiding over there in the corner, admiring you from a distance - may even be a little jealous of Jeff. You know Billy has a crush on you, right? I mean, the guy bought a P-38 just to be near you."

Thomas Willard © 2023

Matt said, "Wes, I've always loved you. Maybe not in all the ways that I love Jeff, but you mean the world to me. You've been like an older brother and have had more impact on my life than you know.

"As far as Billy goes, I think you're right. But he's not just crushing on me; he likes Jeff, too. Jeff and I should have recognized the signs before. Now that we know, and Billy's heard our full story, we'll take him under our wing and help him deal with any suppressed feelings he has and maybe ask Spiegel if he'd be willing to see him." Then the matchmaker in Matt kicked in, and he added, "You know, come to think of it, Linda has a brother that could use a good Wingman.

"Wes, promise, if you ever feel the need to hold me, just give me a call, and I'll be right out. I only live four thousand miles away, and I have a spiffy, newly restored Mustang to fly out here with," and then, as the song finished, Matt hugged Wes with all his might.

Thomas Willard © 2023

Wes, grinning, said, "Don't look now, but I think Jeff saw us hugging and is jealous. Good! I don't want him to ever take you for granted."

Everyone – Linda, Jeff, Mike, Nancy, Wes, and Matt – stayed on the dance floor and came together for the next song, Sam Cooke's "Twistin' the Night Away."

No one was partnered; everyone circulated and danced with whoever they were next to at the moment. But when Matt and Jeff were side-by-side, Jeff noticed Mike and Nancy whisper into Wes' and Linda's ears.

When Jeff mentioned it to Matt, Matt said, "Mike's just like his dad; always a man with a plan."

As the song ended, Nancy rushed to Linda and Mike to Wes, leaving Matt and Jeff to themselves, standing next to each other. Then the next song began, Dinah Washington's "What a Difference a Day Makes."

Jeff, realizing that this was Mike and Nancy's plan, and seeing an embarrassed, deer-in-the-headlights expression on Matt's face, rescued Matt by walking up and putting his arms around him, saying,

"It's OK, Matt. Pretend there's no one else watching, and it's just us, alone in our room at the flak house in Romsey. I've got you, like before," as he held Matt and started to dance.

Matt began to relax and allowed Jeff to lead. Halfway through the song, Matt rested his forehead on Jeff's shoulder to comfort himself but also in an attempt to hide the tears flowing down his face.

After the song ended, Jeff continued to hold Matt to shield him from view while Matt wiped away his tears. Then he hugged Matt with all his might and kissed him on the top of his head before releasing him.

The next song soon started, The Chiffon's latest hit, "One Fine Day," and again, everyone formed into an unpartnered group to dance together. Matt made eye contact with Billy and motioned for him to join them.

Thomas Willard © 2023

Soon after the song began, Jeff, who had been dancing next to and speaking with Linda, let out a loud "Holy cow!" Then after hugging and kissing her, he made a beeline for Matt.

A beaming Jeff pulled Matt into a bear hug and breathlessly said, "Linda just told me she's pregnant."

Matt - flabbergasted - excitedly said, "That's unbelievable, Jeff, congratulations!" and teasingly added, "I always knew you had it in you!"

Jeff, with a knowing smile, replied, "Hey, very funny," and then, grinning from ear to ear, said,

"If it's a boy, which is practically guaranteed with our families, Linda is going to name him Mathew Jeffrey; I don't even get top billing.

"She's adamant, though, so good luck getting her to change her mind," receiving an "Oh, no!" from an at first astonished, then exuberant, and finally contentedly resigned Matt in reply, who was overflowing with immense admiration, love, and joy for his "Forever Wingman."

Thomas Willard © 2023

THE END

Thank you for taking the time to read "Forever Wingman." Please take a moment to rate and review the book; your interest and comments are greatly appreciated.

This concludes the Wingman series. I hope you enjoyed reading the series as much as I enjoyed writing it. As Matt said, "May you always have fair winds and following seas."

Thomas Willard © 2023

www.ingramcontent.com/pod-product-compliance
Lightning Source LLC
LaVergne TN
LVHW020411121224
798954LV00028B/439